ABOUT THE AUTHOR

Winston Xu is a young author living in the United Arab Emirates. Born in China, he moved to Dubai with his family at the age of eight, and soon began writing his first book. He completed Gremword at nine years old. Despite his young age, he has a vivid imagination and a deep love for storytelling. When he's not writing, Winston enjoys reading, playing chess, fencing, and jamming on his guitar. He currently attends primary school in Dubai, where he lives with his parents and little brother.

WINSTON XU

FIRST PRINTING, August 2025.
Harry Markos, Director.

Paperback: ISBN 978-1-917459-97-6
eBook: ISBN 978-1-917459-98-3

Editor: Ian Sharman
Book design by: Ian Sharman
& Winston Xu

www.markosia.com

First Edition

"For My Family,
Special Thanks to My Dear Mother"

WINSTON XU

Contents

Introduction

In the kingdom of Alemis, which was known as the dangerous kingdom, there dwelled hundreds of malevolent creatures, always ready to ambush unsuspecting traders and merchants. However, deep in the heart of the 'Forest of Demons' there lay a lake inhabited by an enormous snake which breathed poisonous fire and had eyes so powerful that it could transform your feeble body into a puddle of water with a single, swift glance. Its scales were as hard as diamond, and the gaps between them as thin as paper. He could grow up to six arms straight out of his mighty skin, holding whatever he wanted them to hold. To slay it, you must have had armour protecting every millimetre of your body, and a sword able to withstand the vicious liquid shot from the tip of its tail. Over the centuries, the people of Alemis had begun to name the mighty, almost invincible beast, Gremword, meaning venom snake.

Alemis itself was a small kingdom covered with countless forests and marshes. In contrast to the size, it had highly populated cities, and Bluriam was only one of the smaller towns.

One
James' Birth

On the opposite side of the Iceshield ocean, standing on the vast landmass of Pareiton, there was a beautiful town called Bluriam. Bluriam was just the perfect place to live, with blacksmiths, carpenters, farmers and a market. But the most important highlight of the small community was the magnificent highway that led all around the coast of Alemis. It was made of stone, but covered with brass that glinted and made it shine. If you followed the bright, yellow trail to the place where it ended, you could just make out the outskirts of the famous Forest of Demons some fifty miles away, a dangerous place where many demons and monsters dwelled. The townspeople of Bluriam had been living peaceful lives for centuries, until a volcano erupted in the Forest of Demons.

That volcano was not one of these little, peaceful-looking ones that did not do much harm, but it was one of those huge ones with boulders and lava spurting out of the top, and mud and rocks rolling down. It was so powerful that the force of it reached the town of Bluriam. In the community, buildings crumbled, stables and stalls collapsed, and halls got burned to ashes.

"Get to the boats!" the headman cried. "The lava flow can't reach us there." The townspeople just had enough time to flee on their small but seaworthy boats. It was not comfortable in the boats, with the fierce wind blowing seawater in everyone's faces, as they could only sail into the Iceshield ocean, but especially for an elegant lady named Evelyn. She was pregnant.

The group of boats stayed well away from the volcano, but it kept on hurling flaming boulders and spitting fire, sending death all the way to the horizon. For months it stayed like that, and Evelyn's belly kept getting more and more painful. Finally, she couldn't stand it anymore, and that evening, on the first day of the last month of the year, Evelyn gave birth to a tough-looking baby with athletic limbs and black hair. Evelyn looked down at him with tears in her eyes, and a smile on her face. As soon as he took his first breath, the baby was already wrapped in warm blankets. After sunset, the only people in the little boat, Evelyn, the baby and a rower, were dozing off. Suddenly, a storm blew out of nowhere. The townspeople were woken up by the noise just in time to see a thirty-metre-high wave racing towards their boats. The wave slammed into the small fleet of boats, wrecking everything and killing everyone. But miraculously, the baby survived, sitting on a splintered piece of wood from the wrecked boat. His fearful eyes saw a pair of hands with sharp, bony fingers rise out of the water, followed by an evil-looking head with hollow eye sockets and jagged front teeth. The head looked at the baby, and quickly dragged him underwater.

The evil creature, a demon, took the baby to an underwater palace on the shallow seabed. The demon had taken the baby because of a prophecy that was foretold years ago, saying that a boy born at the beginning of the last month off the coast of Bluriam would kill the demon lord Gremword. Ever since the prophecy was made, the demons had been checking every single newborn boy in the whole landmass, to see if they were the child of the prophecy. Now that they saw the baby, the demons decided to take him away. The massive underwater palace was five times the size of the Great Pyramid of Giza, and gleamed with gold, diamonds and rare stones. Lanterns lit every tower and turret, and its magical borders glowed faintly. The lawns were covered with crops and rare herbs, with silver roads leading to the great diorite gates. The ceilings of the palace were six to seven metres tall, with hundreds of waterproof candles floating around. The palace contained countless corridors leading to an even larger number of rooms, with the enormous, brightly lit dining hall in the middle of the structure. The baby seemed to be able to breathe underwater, but it was hard for the demon to tell because the baby's strong fists and legs were trying to attack him. When the demon entered the palace, another demon came forward and smiled when he saw what the first demon was holding.

"Nice, Kahtr," he hissed in a grating voice. "You have the child. If we destroy him he will not kill Lord Gremword. The prophecy can be prevented." Kahtr chuckled evilly. "I will tell lord Ravildon about this. He shall be most pleased." Then, he swam off in the direction of the throne room.

Gremword was the demon lord, the ruler of all the demons, but there was a group of other demons that could breathe underwater, and the leader of the underwater demons was called Ravildon. Ravildon's men lived in the underwater palace, unlike the other demons, who lived in the Forest of Demons. Ravildon's ancestors found that they could breathe underwater and see just as well as on land, they chose to live underwater because of their powers, and the Demon Lord at that time agreed. Since then, they had all been living underwater off the coast of Alemis and had built a large palace and established an army. They would also regularly contact the demons living in the Forest, but as they preferred it underwater, they stayed in the beautiful, large undersea palace.

When Kahtr arrived at the throne room, the demon lord Ravildon was just having a late dinner. Kahtr walked into Lord Ravildon's throne room, holding the baby, who was still fighting against his grasp.

"I have taken the baby, lord," Kahtr held out his hands to show Ravildon the baby that he had captured.

"Well done, Kahtr," Ravildon said in a loud, clear voice. "The prophecy will be prevented. Whilst I decide how to destroy him, go put him in the most secure and empty cell that you can find." Kahtr bowed and left the throne room with the baby.

Kahtr took the baby to what looked like a prison cell with stone bars and iron walls. Out of the bars, the baby could just see the borders of the palace. As the titanium doors closed, they made a slight creaking sound, and a second later the door shined brightly, showing that it was locked.

Kahtr left the cell and walked up the deserted corridor full of prison cells. He could hear the loud, furious yelling of some of the prisoners, and grinned to himself. They sounded like they were deathly hungry and almost dead.

Some other cells were quiet, which made Kahtr's grin even wider. They might have already passed out. As he opened a window and jumped out onto the central courtyard, several fish swam by, and he grabbed them with his hands. After slamming them against the palace wall, he shot with amazing speed in the direction of the main palace. When he got in, he saw some people looking uncomfortable and staring away from him when he passed.

"Hey!" Kahtr shouted. "Why're you all looking away from me like I've got a disease! Cheer up, mate." A group of talking ladies suddenly turned away from him, muttering something about babies. Kahtr frowned. Surely no one could be grieving for the child he had imprisoned. He must be the child of the prophecy that would destroy Gremword! Kahtr scowled at a group of frightened-looking cleaners that were scrubbing soap onto the glass panes. Outside on the courtyard, there was a gardener collecting carrots for food that was looking up through the windows at him, before he quickly turned away. Kahtr carried on walking and decided to head to his office next to the Main Gallery, and a large gardening space. Why so many gardening spaces were needed, he did not know.

The next evening, an unusual shark, that seemed to be glowing, swam into the borders of the palace. When it did so, the magical sensors detected the shark, making a large, red tank of lava explode. The sound caused by the explosion caused several demons and mermen to swim towards the shark, which had already reached the freshly mowed lawns. The first tank was connected with other tanks in a line, so the first explosion caused the other tanks to explode. The tanks all exploded, until the seventh tank started to scratch the walls of the palace's library. Then another tank erupted, blowing a hole in one of the walls.

The shark was killed by the next eruption of lava, but there was already a large hole in the walls surrounding the palace's library. Demons and mermen swam out and started to repair the wall, when a mysterious, forceful column of water shot into the library, hitting a bookshelf. It swirled around the bookshelf and hurled it into another bookshelf. Another jet of water, followed by another, knocked dozens of mermen out. Seconds later, three more jets of water sped into the palace and headed towards the baby's cell.

Kahtr heard the action, grabbed his double-sided five-pronged silver trident and streaked off toward the explosions. When he got there, he gasped in surprise as an unseen force knocked him over. He rolled over and jabbed his trident, but only hit thin air. Then, something that looked like a tiny tornado spiralled in his direction, breaking holes in the floor, but Kahtr leaped over it and sent it spinning through the windows. Suddenly, a single file line of soldiers sprinted through a door, wearing aluminium helmets, steel chest-plates and leather boots. In their left hands they held a sturdy shield, and in the right a throwing-trident and a sword. Kahtr followed them in the direction of the shark, but he hadn't gone far when a colossal wall of water engulfed him, and he vanished. Two soldiers stopped in surprise, and suddenly Kahtr's trident clattered onto the floor. The soldiers kneeled down to examine it, and the wall of water killed them too.

In the cell, the baby heard the explosions and saw the mermen swimming towards it. He craned his neck just enough to see the grey shark swimming in the palace's direction. Seconds later, he felt the jets of water racing towards him outside the door, and threw a crab towards the water, but the animal didn't seem to make the water's speed decrease. The water wrapped around the baby, pulling him out of the cell. While the shark was swimming in, Lord Ravildon and other demon generals were eating dinner. The noise caused them to swim towards the action, screaming orders to the merman soldiers.

"What is going on?" Ravildon screamed. Thirty seconds later, when a jet of water came in, a general tried to stop it, but a blur of gold stabbed into the general's chest, reducing him to ashes. The demon lord bellowed with rage, grabbed his trident, and swam into the ocean, accompanied by three demon generals.

Back in the cell, the baby held onto the door handle, but the water seemed to loosen his grip and push him backwards. At that moment, a merman happened to be walking outside and saw the baby pushed by an invisible force, so he started to try to pull the baby back to the cell, but the water's force was too strong. It tugged the baby out of the merman's hands and pulled him around the corner towards the library. At the library, the water was overcoming the mermen and demons, knocking them into the palace, shooting tridents and dragging them into the corals and ocean caves. At one time, a general disappeared behind a glowing ball of water, and none of the demons saw what was happening inside it. Another time, a swirling mass of water whisked away a dozen mermen. Now, after all these attacks, the mermen's numbers were greatly reduced, but the jets of water were still relentlessly attacking the palace.

In the second when three tridents spun out of nowhere, the baby shot into the library with terror in his eyes, pulled by an unseen jet of water. This time, five mermen sped towards the baby, trying to pull him back to the cell, but they were still struggling to prevent the water from dragging the baby away. Eventually, two tridents skewered the mermen, allowing the water to tug the baby away.

"No!" cried a demon. "That baby mustn't go!" but no one listened. They were too busy repairing the library, or desperately trying to not get killed. But at the moment when the baby almost disappeared over a hill of coral, the water seemed to freeze. The tridents stopped halfway towards their targets; balls of water ceased to spiral. Then, all at once the jets of water and tridents seemed to shoot backwards, into the depths of the sea, dropping everything it held, demons, mermen, and the baby. Everyone heard a roar of triumph coming from not far away, and thirty seconds later Ravildon, only flanked by two generals, emerged from a reef. The remaining demons and mermen congratulated their leader for saving the palace, and the demon lord told them that they had blocked the jets of waters' paths and had forced them to change direction. Then the mermen set about repairing the massive gap in the wall, while the demons went back to feasting, celebrating their victory and resting.

While the celebration was happening, the baby was instantly pulled back to his small, lonely cell by two mermen, who had a stronger and a firmer grip on him, fearing any further attacks, while another merman carrying his trident and a shield swam behind. The shield was sprinkled with diamond and forged of diorite, making it a strong defence against more tridents. The original titanium door was destroyed by the jets of water, so not a long time after it was replaced by a new, steel door. When this door locked, it made a louder and a lower creaking sound. This door was more stable and was less likely to collapse. Even after the door was locked and when the sea was peaceful, the mermen looked out the glass windows of the corridor and listened to the baby for a long time before turning to leave.

In the palace's dining hall, long, splendid tables were set in four rows lengthways, packed with delicious food and magnificent drinks. There was roast boar stuffed with carrot and rice, pigeons almost covered with fantastic spices, and small plates scattered around, holding several kinds of vegetables. Mermen bustled around, serving more amazing dishes of appetising food, or bringing around jugs of rich, red wine. Ravildon sat at the head table with his most trusted generals and advisors, who were all enjoying the juiciest meat, the tastiest sauces, and the very best drinks. After fifty minutes of the fine food, the deserts came. The tables were completely covered as before, but this time with macarons, baklavas, ice creams, and cake.

When everyone was full, Ravildon stood up.

"Good evening, everyone," he said, "welcome to this evening's feast." Then, seeing that all the demons and mermen were focused, he continued, "I have decided that we will need a few improvements for our palace." A few mermen shuffled around in their benches. "As you all know, today we have experienced an attack," he said. "I cannot and will not pretend that it has not caused severe damage to our palace's walls. In the future, we must always be prepared and ready for an attack like this. Starting from tomorrow, we will establish a safer and better security system for this place. It shall contain fireproof cameras, capturing images of anybody or anything that enters our borders, and clear evidence of any crime. These images will be clearly seen on an efficient device that will be set in the control room." He paused and then announced, "Our palace also deserves a proper defence system, with high-speed sensors and guns firing energy and lighting, all set on towers around the borders. Anything that survives the guns will be trapped by a spiked net, which will then drag the bodies and weapons of the attackers into a tren-..." At that moment, a humming sound started, and strangely it seemed to come from everywhere, under tables, in the walls, behind benches... Ravildon hesitated, uncertainly looking at everyone and everywhere, the mermen and demons did the same. Then, the noise grew louder, and the pitch grew higher, and then suddenly everyone heard ten loud sounds. They turned as one towards the head table, just in time to see that their leader and eight other generals and advisors were clutching their heads, their thighs and their stomachs, where bullets had pierced them. Everyone started running everywhere, screaming in terror, demons and mermen alike, tripping over each other.

Two
A New Home

In the confusion, no one noticed as ten short, slender figures wearing light brown robes crawled into the shadows. They were armed with two long daggers and slings, with five missiles each. The figures were Fesittes, a tribe of people who lived in the ocean, far away from Ravildon, because they were enemies of the demons. In the past few centuries, they'd had small conflicts together, and the rivalry had intensified over time. The Fesittes were preparing for their second assault on the huge palace. The first attack with the shark was to simply weaken the defences, and to allow part of the actual army to advance into the palace. They had now defeated the mermen in the library and had stormed into the dark rooms and the sombre corners of the palace, tackling the passing mermen and demons. As the civilian mermen and demons fled from the dining hall, they became aware of the groups of armed Fesittes hiding in the shadows. Many demons died from the short attacks from the highly trained Fesitte soldiers.

Meanwhile, in the dining hall, the Fesittes with slings were joined by some Fesitte archers. They crept around the hall, shooting their long, green-shafted arrows at demon generals, who were the only ones remaining in the dining hall. Ravildon had darted out of the dining hall, and was trying to organise the mermen into groups and escort the demons who were not soldiers back into their suites. The generals were now trying to find the archers, but it was very difficult as the archers were sneaking and creeping around and communicating in low voices. Finally, an archer said something too loud, so a general heard him and cried, "One's there!" The archers became aware of the generals running towards them, so they swiftly devised a tactic. They formed two ranks and began to fire with less accuracy, pretending to be panicking. While the generals were attacking the ranks, three more archers snuck up from behind and shot the generals. The generals realised that they were defeated, only two demon generals managed to escape from the arrows and inform the demon lord.

In the palace the Fesitte troops formed five groups, with the archers on the inside. They moved into the inner part of the palace and made a circle around the dining hall and the kitchens, where the most people were. The palace's mermen soldiers started to form defensive ranks, but these were badly organised and were easily broken by the attackers. However, none of the attackers knew that there was an army of a million mermen all wearing armour and armed with shields and tridents under the seabed, who were always ready for attacks and only needed seconds of preparation. What the demons and mermen didn't know was that their beautiful palace was besieged by another million Fesittes.

Suddenly, trapdoors opened from all around the palace. Thousands of mermen poured out of secret rooms and halls under the seabed. They formed circles around the small number of Fesitte troops, outnumbering the attackers in the palace. But when the attackers seemed to have failed, missiles started to pierce the palace's ceiling from the second floor. Boulders, burning wood, and dead bodies poured from the ceiling, causing many wooden planks to crash into the floor. Again, bits of the floor collapsed, raining rubble on top of the fleeing mermen.

But more trap doors opened, and thousands more heavily armed merman soldiers ran out and started to fix the holes in the ceiling. These soldiers were always ready for surprise attacks like this one, as a gigantic palace like this one always needed lots of soldiers. Yet, without warning, the front and side doors had started to creak.

Bang! The large, heavy stone doors that lead into the palace broke. The first thing the demons saw were two huge, heavy metal battering rams topped with gold; both were used by four Fesittes. The Fesittes were a species of humans with water powers, and the army's commander was the imprisoned baby's father, although the baby didn't know that. Behind each battering ram stood two hundred more Fesittes, armed with tridents, daggers and shields, and they were all wearing armour. They advanced into the palace from multiple sides, hacking down walls, setting tables on fire, duelling and shooting the demons, who were still swarming out of the trapdoors. The palace had become a battlefield.

At the front of the dining hall, armed mermen were moving out in all directions, escorting demons to their rooms and suites. But even with the merman escorts, many demons died from missiles or attacks. The Fesittes attacked from two or more directions, and arrows slew the mermen while they are distracted. The wounded Ravildon swam around, killing Fesittes as he went, but more of them kept coming. His forces also seemed to be slightly overwhelmed by the Fesittes, as they were surprised by the sudden assault. When the mermen and demons were almost defeated, the Fesittes' weapons seemed to sail backwards. The mermen and demons were pushed forward and attacked the Fesittes with newfound strength; Ravildon was using his powers to defeat the Fesittes. The demons and mermen pushed the

Fesittes back towards the doors, with more rising to join them. Then, the mermen pursued the Fesittes back to the doors, and into the palace's fields. They rained tridents onto the Fesittes, killing a Fesitte with each blow. The Fesittes retreated almost to the palace's borders, with a large number hurt or dead.

Suddenly, the sea lit up above the palace. No one had noticed the commander of the Fesitte army above, surveying the scene. Now, he sped down to the palace, blasting holes with his gigantic, golden trident. He had brown eyes, and his brown beard was long but tied in a bun to prevent anyone from pulling it. He seemed to be sprinting when he swam, with his legs kicking the water above. Beside him, there were five tridents, all flowing to his will. He landed on the vast green fields and directed his troops to use a new tactic. As his troops slashed at the enemies, he fought his way through the enemy lines into the palace. The commander shot flames at walls, skewered demons, and destroyed whole rooms. He was trying to find the demon lord Ravildon, and to overcome him in single combat. He swam towards the kitchens and searched the entire dining hall, but Ravildon was still nowhere to be seen.

Suddenly, as he entered one of the corridors closer to the baby's cell, green light filled the room. Unexpectedly, Ravildon appeared right in front of the Fesitte commander's face, holding his massive golden trident, with his face contorted in fury.

"So, you came," growled Ravildon. "You shall pay for this damage."

"I will never pay. You will be the one who pays, and you will now bring me the child that you have imprisoned," replied the commander. Without giving the demon lord time to react, he briefly feinted and then stabbed at his arm, but Ravildon dodged the blow, grabbed the Fesitte commander's wrist and slashed his trident at the commander's face, but the commander was just as fast. His eyes glowed, and the water around him shot at the demon lord from multiple angles. At the same time, the commander deflected the demon lord's trident and kicked him in the chest. The demon lord was pushed back, and slammed into a magnificent, emerald crystal chandelier. In front of him, the commander slammed the butt of his trident into the demon lord's stomach and stamped his foot. Immediately the water released the demon lord, and he slumped onto the ground.

The Fesitte commander raised his trident, ready to kill the demon lord, but the demon lord's eyes suddenly opened. He grabbed his trident and scrambled out of the way before the trident could hit him. The trident missed an inch from the demon lord's elbow, and it hit the hard stone ground. Because of that, the commander lost his balance, so the demon lord punched the Fesitte commander in the face and pinned him to the ground.

He knocked the trident out of his hand, stabbed him in the arm and laughed.

"You will never defeat me, you little idiot and your army of fools. I win every game I play." Yet when the demon lord was laughing, the commander saw his chance, punched the demon lord and used water to press him. The commander's eyes lit up, and water pushed the demon lord up to the ceiling and slammed him to the floor. Then he got hurled to the end of the corridor, right onto a pair of titanium double doors. A millisecond later, the demon lord screamed, and a trident appeared in his leg. Then, a net fell on his head and wrapped up his body like a cocoon. A moment later, the net turned into an iron cage, and glowed. The demon lord had been captured.

Behind the iron net stood a Fesitte general and two Fesitte soldiers. The commander looked around and said, "Well, the plan has worked. Good job, general."

The general nodded. "The demons have retreated into their kitchens and the dining hall. The other troops are about to finish them off."

"I'll go there immediately," the commander said. "You guys try to get the child. You might be able to open the cell's door with your water powers." With that, the commander, the general and the soldiers sped off in different directions. The commander arrived when the demons were giving their last efforts. What remained of their troops were being pushed back against the walls and were giving their final attempts to wound some Fesittes. The Fesitte troops didn't have a lot of remaining warriors either, but at least they had more numbers than the demons. The commander's tactics were working, even now. As the commander entered the dining hall, a section of the wall broke and ten Fesitte troopers rushed in and surrounded a rank of demons. The commander yelled more orders to his men, and with those new tactics they attacked the exhausted, injured demons and mermen even more efficiently. The commander caused five tridents to slay their owners, skewered five demons, and deflected three blows at once. Finally, the demons saw that they had lost, turned and fled. The Fesittes pursued them all the way to the borders of the palace, but then let them flee.

The general was able to break the small but heavy steel door. They hauled the baby out of the cell, but he thought they were just more demons. The Fesitte soldiers were also struggling to carry the baby, who was pummelling the Fesittes with his fists. The Fesittes finally brought the baby to the commander in the demons' dining hall, which had become a simple hospital. The wounded Fesittes were being healed and bandaged by some medics. The net containing the demon lord lay in a corner, beside two soldiers. The Fesitte general brought the baby straight to the commander, who was sitting on a massive, ocean blue chair, the seat of the demon lord. Two Fesitte generals stood beside him, in deep conversation. However, as soon as the baby arrived, he stood up in front of his seat and cradled him in his arms.

The commander looked at his son for the first time in his life. There were tears in his eyes as he looked at his son's brown eyes and black hair. The baby had double eyelids, just like the commander. The baby had also stopped crying and was gazing at the commander with wide eyes.

"Sorry for not saving you sooner," whispered the commander sadly. After a long time, the commander looked up. "For now, we need to give my son rest and food. Then, when everyone's ready we will head back to my palace," he said and handed the baby to the general, who bowed.

"Yes, sir!" Then, the general swam with the baby into a side room with walls of bronze. Inside the room, there was a bed with red blankets, and a basket of fish and fruit beside the bed. The general told the baby to eat some food, and instantly the baby started to tuck in. He was very hungry after two days in the cell.

After twenty minutes, the commander gathered up his remaining troops. He was holding his baby in his arms, and he announced that the Fesittes would now be departing to a teleporter. The commander had a map of where every teleporter was, so he knew where to go. Teleporters were portals that could teleport a person or an object to another teleporter, and these were essential travelling structures for the undersea peoples. Teleporters have doors made of coral, leading to a small room. On the floor was a portal that transports something to another teleporter's portal, and on the walls were maps of where the other teleporters were. To be transported to where you want to go, you just jumped in the portal and said your destination, and after a few seconds you would arrive. The Fesittes travelled for thirty minutes to the closest teleporter and teleported to their underwater palace in twos and threes, which took another ten minutes.

Finally, everyone was at the gigantic, golden gates of the humongous palace. The palace was a massive, turquoise complex on the seabed, with fortified walls and the highest level of security. The complex was made of several teleporters, galleries, fields, rooms, small bases, palaces and arenas. There were brightly lit houses for the servants and yellow pyramids and entertainment centres scattered around. Roofed corridors went from structure to structure, crisscrossing the green fields. In the middle of the complex was the palace itself. The Fesittes marched into the palace and into the dining hall, where they were greeted by the guards and lady Fesittes. There was a huge feast that was even grander than the one at the demons' palace, and a party around the whole complex. All the time the commander's son was either hugged by the commander or sitting on a silver chair that moved around by itself. The celebration went on all through the day, and well into the night. At last, it was time to sleep. The Fesittes all went back to their rooms and started to rest.

The next day, there was a speech in one of the halls. The hall was huge, with hundreds of rows of bronze chairs facing a raised platform. When everyone was seated, the commander stood onto the platform and cleared his throat.

"As you all know, we have had a massive battle against Ravildon's demons and won. The reason for that battle was to retrieve my newborn child, who was taken." The Fesittes in front of him gasped as he revealed his baby, who was under a blanket. "However," he continued, "even though we have won, we must always be ready to defend our palace complex against a counterattack. Our defences must be tightened! The demons will want revenge." After a short pause, he delivered the final part of the short speech, "In the meantime, my child is to be in a private suite of rooms that no one else will enter, except for myself, and this group of people here, who will always take care of him." He indicated a teacher, a cook, two hunters, and soldiers.

After the speech, everyone went about their normal business, except for the baby, the commander, and the group that the commander had indicated during the speech. They met in a room in one of the corners of the palace, which was normally used for storage. The commander said, "I don't want anyone else to know about this, but I would like you to raise my baby in the cave I showed you yesterday, on that island. As you know, I fear that the demons might recruit and launch an attack on us, and I cannot risk having him taken again. I am unable to raise him, as I may be needed in this palace complex. The cave is not big, but if you step under the largest stalactite a pathway will open. There is a kitchen, nine beds, a storage room, a couch, two washrooms and two spare rooms. There will be everything you need to raise him. Raise him for ten years and send a message to me if anything is wrong, and don't let him near the cliff. Does everybody understand?"

"Do we really need to raise him for ten years?" a soldier muttered, but the commander heard him.

"I said, raise him for ten years!" The commander shouted. No one asked any more questions. "Then I don't see any reason why you shouldn't get going!" After that, the teacher, who was carrying the baby, and all the other Fesittes started swimming towards the closest teleporter and teleported straight towards the cave.

Three
Assault by the Demons

NINE YEARS LATER

For nine years, the ten Fesittes raised the baby. Every day, they took the baby, who had started to grow into a young child, and taught him swordplay, hunting, how to speak and survival skills. Every night, as the child was sleeping, the five adult soldiers armed with tridents took shifts guarding the cave, looking out for sneaky demon soldiers creeping towards it. They lived like this for nine years, and no demons found them. Once in a while, the soldiers could hear some demonic voices whispering behind a wall of hard, strong rock, but they never got inside their cave, until one night when the child was nine. The Fesittes had come up with a name for the him when he was three - James. They had decided that it should be a human name, so humans would not find him strange.

James was sleeping peacefully one night, when the soldier on guard heard someone banging his shield on the stony wall. He quickly alerted the hunters and the other soldiers, who always kept their weapons close at hand.

"It's them all right," a hunter whispered. "Seems like there's a lot of them. Maybe they won't hear you if you keep your voice down and if you stop banging your trident."

"I wasn't banging it," The soldier looked offended. "And maybe they won't hear you if you keep your mouth shut!"

The hunter stamped his foot, causing the other hunter to tell him to stop making noise. But a demon seemed to have noticed something behind the rock, as he'd started telling his comrades to gather. Soon, there were several

31

shields and tridents banging against the rock, trying to heave the boulders apart to clear a path.

"Damn it," the hunter said. "Now that they know where we are, they'll be on us any second!"

"Oh, so it's now my fault," the soldier shouted.

"Stop it!" yelled another soldier. "We need to be ready when the enemy approaches. You hunters have bows, so dip the arrows in poison and hide behind those boulders there to be safe when you shoot. Soldiers, three at the rocks, two go behind them and form two ranks."

In ten seconds, the Fesittes were ready with their weapons. They were just in time, because at that time the last boulder was rolled away. At the front were two demons behind shields. They pushed through the mass of small rocks and bashed their shields against the first soldier, but the hunters were ready immediately. They nocked, drew and fired in less than a second, and their arrows soared high above the Fesittes and into the demons' heads. One demon managed to raise his shield, but his companion got an arrow in his neck. He buckled and fell face down on a sharp rock. The hunters already had fresh arrows, but there was no need. They shot right as the three soldiers slammed their tridents into the remaining demon. One trident and two arrows skewered and slew the demon, who crashed into the demon behind. However, the Fesittes soon realised that there were much more demons behind.

"Get through at once, and we can overwhelm them!" the demon centurion screamed. "They don't have a lot of men!" Without warning, four more boulders toppled down. As the soldiers jumped back in alarm, four demons darted into the cave, but the hunters' arrows intercepted them. Both hunters launched two arrows at once, and three of the arrows hit their targets. But, unfortunately, two of the arrows hit the same demon, so only two demons were hit. In fact, one of the arrows only scraped a demon's stomach, and he could still fight. At this time the two Fesittes that were behind came forward, and the battle levelled out again.

All the noise woke James. He got up and heard fighting nearby. When he investigated, he saw that their cave was being attacked. Luckily, he was quite good at fighting himself, so he grabbed a knife and ran into the battle. The two remaining Fesittes had also woken up and ran into the fight with kitchen knives. The two soldiers that came forward were now forming a semicircle around the gap, pushing the demons with their shields and stabbing them with the short swords they always carried on their belts. James arrived just as the hunters released new, fresh arrows. One was aimed at a demon's face, and one at his neck. The shots went home, and a demon went down. But these arrows were met by three more arrows from the gap - the demons also had archers! The three shots from the demons were aimed in the direction where the Fesitte hunters were, but they were too clever to stay in the same place. They briskly crawled behind a larger boulder, ducked under the arrows and nocked their own arrows. James dodged the enemy arrows and raced towards the gap. A demon had thrown his weapon at a Fesitte. It didn't hit him, but the Fesitte staggered backward. James saw his chance, stepped to the left of the demon and stabbed him briefly, before the demon could raise his shield. Then James slid between the demon's legs and cut the demon's leg twice. Next, a Fesitte soldier hit the demon with his shield, and he went down.

James skidded to a stop just as the hunters shot new arrows. One was caught on a stone, centimetres beside a demon, but the other arrow hit the demon in his knee. Still on his hands and knees, James crawled to the other side of the gap, skidded into throwing range, and hurled the sharp, prolonged blade into a demon's neck, which was only shielded by a thin layer of leather. Then, James retrieved his knife, leaped upward, and sliced off the demon's arm. He flipped in the air and landed on two tremendous boulders. Next, James used the power of his legs to propel him towards another rock, kicked and soared into the air, narrowly missing a few enemy arrows, but now the Fesittes were backing away into the depths of the cave, and more demons were coming! Thinking quickly, James cut off two stalactites in mid-air and threw his knife at the demons below him. At the same time, the hunters shot two arrows at the demons, and they both hit their marks - a knee and an eye. James pushed against the wall, and the force sent him shooting down at a forty-five-degree angle. As he hit the ground, he kicked once more, and James propelled himself into one of the spare rooms, which had nothing but a weapon rack in it. James glanced at the weapons - three spears, a trident, five shields, a spare quiver of arrows and a sword. James selected a spear and dashed back into the battle.

At the fight, the Fesittes were retreating. The demons had pushed forward with greater strength and more arrows. The hunters had sped off for more arrows, and that left only five Fesittes against an almost endless stream of demons. James kicked on the wall and flew into the air, stabbed twice and then spun his spear around. The spear knocked down a spiral of stalactites, but only one or two hit demonic flesh. The teacher and the cook weren't doing too well; they were rapidly retreating, and mainly focused on defending themselves. James saw that they needed help and rushed to their aid. spinning through the air, he used his spear like a quarterstaff, twirling it, knocking off weapons, slashing across flesh, parrying blows. He finally reached the cook, hit the ground with his spear, backflipped and drove one end of his spear into an enemy's shoulder. He screamed as he fell. James then spun his spear in front of him. The demons there went down too, so he made a series of quick cuts and stabs at his opponents and took off. In the air, it looked as if he just cut a slice of a cake, but the cake refilled itself immediately.

The hunters arrived with thirty new arrows. They shot five each in three seconds, and seven demons went down. James pushed the wall, just as the hunters both shot three more arrows. Five demons went down. James was so distracted by the scene on the floor that he landed in the middle of the demons, but then he swept his spear in a wide circle, knocking off balance all the demons there. He picked up a demon's dagger, threw it, and skewered two demons who were planning to catch him on his back. Then, James scooped up three more daggers, threw one and parried every other strike. Then he killed five demons, injured seven and at last he had fought his way to a wall. He kicked at it, then at the ground, and he propelled himself to the ceiling! While the demons were yelling at him to come down, he sent down a hail of stalactites, but only for them to be intercepted by a volley of arrows. James leapt back toward the Fesittes.

With the Fesittes retreating, more demons had managed to pour in and attack at once. There were so many, it seemed endless. With so many coming at once, the demons could attack at more places, and the Fesittes simply couldn't deflect every stab and slash at once. A demon managed to stab a soldier on his arm, and another Fesitte had a cut on his leg. The hunters kept sending volley after volley of arrows into the enemy, but these arrows were greeted by returning volleys from the demons. James kept flying through the air and killing demons, but all the Fesittes' efforts weren't enough to repel them. The continuous stream just kept flowing and flowing. Now the cave was full of arrows, spiked stones, dead bodies, and blood. Every time a demon fell, another took his place. Although these demons could not wield their weapons too well, their force was endless.

On the other hand, James' body seemed to be set on automatic. He slashed, cut, rolled and stabbed without thinking, and with absolute ease. Combat was a power he had inherited from his father, the army's commander and the tribe's leader. The higher his rank was, the more powerful he was. However, the soldiers and hunters were panicking. The teacher and the cook had both fallen, due to multiple wounds, leaving the rest to a larger ring of demons. Three of the soldiers and a hunter were thinking of an escape plan.

"The other soldiers and a hunter can accompany James away," a soldier said in a low voice. "Then us and the remaining hunter will stay here for a while, wait until we think they are far away, then we get back to our palace. That way, they're unlikely to get James. We don't know if they've been hiding behind special forces." He raised his shield to deflect two arrows and a stab.

"Good idea, if they don't get us instead."

"They won't. We're just here for a short while."

"But how are the others going to know?" asked a soldier.

"We'll just pass it on," replied the soldier, who parried another sword stroke. Soon, every soldier and the two hunters all knew about the plan.

"But how is James going to know?" asked a hunter, as he shot down three demons. Then without warning, the floor began to rumble. A bunch of stronger and bigger demons burst from the gap and started attacking with their massive battle axes and shields. "We can't handle this by ourselves," yelled that hunter over the noise. "We need to report to the commander! We can use the lightning messaging thing on your trident to inform him."

"I'll try it," a soldier shouted. He spun his trident in a circle and stabbed it into the ground.

Four
Escape to the Future

After a while in the palace, the commander was sitting on his throne enjoying molten lava cake, when the bolt of lightning sent from the cave arrived and turned into the shape of a man.

"Commander," it said hurriedly, "the cave and your son are being attacked by demons," and dissolved into water. The commander was surprised to hear that the demons were able to find the cave, and why they wanted his son so much.

"Demons? Why are they here again?" he asked, and quickly said to a servant, "Tell general Ryker to organise a force of fifty soldiers and fifteen trained archers and tell him that it is an emergency. Ask Bernard to get suitable weapons for fighting on land." Bernard was a head servant who worked at the armoury.

After the servant was gone, he started off towards one of his private storage rooms. It was a huge room, with five desks in the middle, seven maps on the far end, a chandelier on the ceiling and the walls were dotted with barrels, chests and cabinets. But he ignored everything except for a patch of the floor in front of the smallest map. He spoke a password, and the floor opened into a hole, with a ladder leading down into it. The commander closed the trapdoor as he descended the ladder. At the foot of the ladder was a black trident. He picked it up and slowly stretched his foot into the tunnel, as if scared of a trap. Then, the floor opened before him, to reveal a gigantic cauldron of bubbling liquid. He tossed the trident into the liquid, stepped over the cauldron and started walking. The trident needed enchantments and special powers from the liquid.

At last, he came to a humongous hall lit by three chandeliers. There was a burning fire in the centre of the room, surrounded by two chairs and a stool. At both ends of the hall were two enormous thrones made of basalt and ringed with silver, and on both sides of each throne were two barrels. The commander approached the throne on the right and opened the barrel on the left. Inside the barrel was the same black trident that he had discarded into the cauldron of bubbling liquid, but it was glowing and was ringed with gold and had diamond on the tips on the blades. He picked it up and opened the other chest. Lying inside was a glowing iron sword, with a golden handle and its blade covered with a layer of platinum. Beside the sword was a leather scabbard decorated with elegant patterns, and a leather belt of the same quality. The commander put on the belt and the scabbard, sheathed his sword and held his trident, and sat on the throne. For a moment, nothing happened. Then, the throne flashed three times, and the commander slammed the butt of his trident into the ground. With a blinding flash of blue, the commander disappeared.

The commander reappeared in front of a teleporter, on the seabed. The throne was the only teleporter that could teleport to this one, and only the commander knew that. But this teleporter was unique. It was made of metal and covered with pins and screws. The sea around the teleporter was also different. It was polluted and was covered by a layer of plastic bottles and bags, and the acid made it smelly. Scattered among the rubbish were dead bodies of fish, some of which were already rotten and had bones and flesh falling off. The commander swam to the surface. When he looked at the sky, he could just make out the tiny dot that was a helicopter. He had teleported to the future. The commander walked to the shore of a nearby island. He could simply float around and walk whenever he was at the surface of a body of water. The commander arrived at the foot of a tall cliff, but he had no trouble getting over it. In fact, he didn't climb over it, he went through it. He slammed his trident into the firm rock, and strolled up its side, sliding his trident along as he went. The commander stopped about halfway up. He unsheathed his sword and tapped it twice on the rock. The rock opened up to a tunnel, and he entered. The tunnel was dimly lit by a few lanterns here and there, but it was an empty void. The commander picked up his pace to a run. Further down the tunnel it became darker. The commander started to sprint. Suddenly a brick wall appeared in front of him, and he skidded to a stop. But when he stabbed the brick wall twice and slashed at it with his sword, the wall flashed gold and began to crumble...

Suddenly, the tunnel became bright with a sudden blast of noise and light and nature. It was a completely different atmosphere to the sombre tunnel and the disgusting ocean, and a much cleaner smell. As he looked around, the commander saw that he was inside a jungle, but with only a thin layer of trees and undergrowth. Birds were tweeting and monkeys were crawling in the trees. Butterflies and insects buzzed and flew around, circling around plants, landing on flowers. A brown path went around the trees, and the commander followed it, until he reached the edge of the forest, where he stopped and looked around. The path continued in a straight line, down the mountain. It ended in the middle of a ring of mountains. It was like a huge crater, or the hole in the middle of a volcano.

And standing in the middle of the ring of mountains was a complex of structures and fields with roofed corridors leading from one place to another, surrounded by steep tree-covered cliffs and mountains. There was a low wall surrounding it, and a few guard posts, which was covered with vines and undergrowth, to make it camouflaged with the jungle background. About halfway down the walls was a gate, which was guarded by four Fesittes. The commander walked to the gate, the guards were suspicious of him, but they relaxed when they saw who it was.

"Commander, why are you here?" a Fesitte guard asked.

"My son was unsafe in the secret cave," he said. "The demons have found him after nine years. I have decided to hide him here, in the future, with other children who are unsafe. This way he will be able to have proper training.

"I see he isn't with you, so when will he be arriving?"

The commander glared at him. "After I return to normal time and get him," he said. "Now return to your duty, Maxon." The man called Maxon went back to his post. Next, the commander entered the town. There were lots of buildings and areas for activities such as archery, swordplay, rock climbing and sprinting. Other buildings were for dining, resting, sleeping and for the adults to do work. The commander headed for a small cabin at the far end of it, with the symbol of an eagle drawn on the door. He gently tapped twice at the door.

"Come in," grunted a gruff voice. The commander opened the door to a small room, with two chairs, a table, a shelf, a bed and a smaller door leading to a toilet. Sitting on a chair was a muscular man that was slightly above the average height, with long, brown hair and black eyes. He was poring over a book of notes and recordings, adding new notes to it.

"Good morning, Cordova," the commander said. The man looked up.

"Good morning, commander," said Cordova. "May I ask why you are here?"

"My son is coming here. He is nine years old, and according to some of my soldiers, he is quite good with a knife, a sword or a spear. He just can't do archery, so you guys should train him more in that."

General Cordova added some more notes. "Any more stuff I need to know?"

"Save a place for him in room No. 2." Rooms one and two were the largest and the fanciest, and only children of commanders or leaders could live there. Then the commander returned to his palace, took his trident and swam off to the cave.

At the cave, the new arriving soldiers had startled the demons. In a few seconds, seventeen arrows were already arcing through the air, and thirteen demons went down. Twenty arrows came from the demons, but these shots were not accurate, and none hit their marks. The soldiers with no bows formed two ranks and held their spears right above the original soldiers' shoulders, held their shields at a diagonal angle and pushed forward, stabbing their spears at the demons. James was flying around, raining stalactites, but the stalactites were running out. There were only a few of them left, so James decided to go down. He landed in the middle of the demons, opening three cuts rapidly in a demon's chest as he landed. Then he slid between three pairs of legs, slicing them off. Then he rose to his feet, and stabbed three times at the demon behind him, kicked the demon in front of him and sent him sprawling onto the tip of a Fesitte soldier's spear. The line of spears then hit a shield wall made by the demons. The Fesittes swiftly drew their swords, leaped upward or ducked down, and slashed their legs or stabbed at their heads. Most of the demons in their front rank went down, but then the stronger demons were in front of the Fesittes. They were three hands taller than the Fesittes and two hands more than normal demons, but they were only wilder and dumber. James attacked them at the back, while the Fesitte soldiers stabbed them with their spears. Although the demons' shields were big and they had battle axes, they couldn't deflect too many stabs at once and their heavy axes were easy to avoid. Finally, the last of the demons had been killed.

The Fesittes and James made it back to the underwater palace, where the commander was waiting for them at the gates.

The commander called, "James!" It was the first time that he had seen him in nine years. The commander and James hugged each other for a few minutes. Then the commander looked up. "Soldiers and hunters, you can return to your rooms or your duties." The Fesitte soldiers and the hunters marched into the palace. "James, you can follow me. I don't want anyone else to know, but you need a safer place to live. I have decided to bring you to a secret jungle base, where you will get proper training."

"Then why didn't you bring me there in the first place? A town sounds a lot better than a cave, and I was a baby."

"As you said, you were a baby. That camp's training is for teenagers. There is no easy mode or baby mode on anything, if you're bad at it. Everyone goes through the same process of training and learning," the commander told him.

"Whatever," said James, "but the demons found me in the cave. Then how come they can't find me in the jungle base?"

"It is not just in a jungle," the commander said. "It is a hidden town with a wall that can only be opened by specific tridents and swords, and that if you had the wrong weapon, you would fall into lava. And most importantly of all, it is in the future."

Meanwhile, the demon generals had just heard about the soldiers failing to take James.

"Dammit! So, you're telling me that you failed again, after NINE YEARS?!" Abaddon, a general for the evil demon emperor Gremword, bellowed. They were in his base in the Forest of Demons, and a messenger had just reported the news. "What will Gremword, the emperor, say? You already found him so how did you NOT DEFEAT THEM?" The messenger demon staggered back in alarm.

"They were too many! They had skilled archers, and then a relief force came!"

"Archers? I thought we also had archers! We had so many men, how could a relief force defeat us? Oh no, now he is going to the future. Gremword might be killed!"

The messenger swayed on his feet. "Y-your ex-exe-excellency, th-there was no-nothing I could d-do about it!"

"Now go away!" Abaddon roared, causing the messenger to scamper off. "What will happen now?" Abaddon asked himself angrily and worriedly. "I must see the priest." He briskly ran into a corridor at his right, arrived at the end of it, turned left, walked a few metres and tapped twice at a door.

"Come in," a calm voice spoke slowly. Abaddon opened the door, and found himself facing a man with a long, black beard. His eyes were shining yellow.

"Nine years ago, you gave me the prophecy that a child will kill the emperor Gremword when he grows up. Now, he is heading to the future. What do you predict will happen now?"

"You should've killed him. The child, called James, will eventually kill Gremword, and there's no stopping him anymore. He and two friends will journey through the forest to Gremword's palace," the priest predicted. Abaddon, having heard the news, was so shocked that he didn't close the door. He just darted back to his throne room.

Five
The Base

Meanwhile in the Fesitte commander's palace, the commander was leading James toward the teleporter to the future. James kept asking questions, like "How big is that place?" and "What do they have there?" until the cauldron of bubbling liquid appeared. As the commander tossed the trident in, James asked, "Why is that pot blocking our way?" The commander smiled as it faded away, as fast as it came.

"It's okay to walk now. We'll need the trident later; it just needs a special power from the liquid." At last, they arrived at the hall. James followed his father toward the throne on the right and watched him take the weapons out of the barrels. "Now, we get on the throne together, at the same time. This is actually a teleporter to the future. The one opposite goes to the past. When you are in the future, stay close to me. Understand?"

"Understand."

"Good," the commander said. "Sit on it now!" James and his father sat on the enormous throne at once, which flashed three times and teleported them to the future.

When they arrived in the future, two thousand years later at the bottom of the ocean, James and the commander swam up to the surface of the ocean.

"Wow," James exclaimed. "This world looks so cool! There are boats that move without oars over there, and that buzzing bird up above." Then he spotted the island. "What's on there?" The commander smiled again and told James to follow him to the side of the island, where there was a tall cliff. Then, as the tunnel appeared, James asked, "Does that lead to the jungle base?" The commander told him to pick up his pace, and that James was correct. After the commander had climbed up to the desired height, with James holding his hand, they sprinted until the wall appeared, skidded to a stop, the commander slashed at the wall with the sword from the barrel, and as the wall crumbled to dust the sudden blast of nature and light and noise surprised James. It was a completely different atmosphere. And facing them, was the picturesque jungle base. James stared at the sight. It was magnificent, he thought. A secret jungle complex with natural fortifications? That was extremely cool. Then the commander approached the gate, and Maxon stepped forward.

"Good morning. A space has been saved for your son in room two. I hope he has a good time here." Then he looked at James. "James, welcome to our base. Breakfast is at sunrise, lunch at noon and dinner after sunset. You will have several other children in your room, but everyone has their own sleeping bags and toiletries. Have a great time!" And with that, Maxon returned to his post.

As the commander led James through the corridors of the sun-lit town, James goggled at every building, field and plant. "What's that?" he would ask. Finally, they reached the rooms. The rooms were huge. They were arranged in a line, and each room had a sign hanging over them - the numbers from one to twenty. Each room was of equal size, but the smaller numbers were made of more expensive material; one and two were made of gold and diamond and decorated with precious stones. Each room was about ten by seven metres big. When he entered room two, James found a spare sleeping bag and a sack of toiletries and clothes piled up in the corner under a lantern. Around it, there were loads of other sleeping bags and sacks lying around.

As James tidied up his stuff, the commander said, "Goodbye, son. I hope that you will have a good time here." James stood up and ran to hug him.

"Goodbye!" he said. Then the commander kissed James and left the room.

After James had finished laying out his sleeping bag, it was already time for dinner at the dining pergola. In the pergola, there were twenty-one tables, twenty for the children from different rooms and the last one for the staff. Cordova was sitting at the staff table, and as the last of the children and teenagers filed in, he stood up behind his chair. As James glanced at his empty plate and goblet, he wondered what he would eat. Then Cordova spoke.

"Good evening, everyone. Our meal will start in a few minutes." James had just noticed how hungry he was. "But first, we will welcome a new child to our base: James, son of the commander of the Fesittes!" A round of quiet applause. "Now, we shall start the feast. Tell the invisible servants what you want, and they'll bring it to you! Have a nice feast!"

Clean, paper menus appeared on their plates. James was not sure if it would work, but as the person sitting beside him yelled, "Spaghetti," James said, "Roast chicken drumsticks," and a plate of chicken legs appeared in front of him.

The person sitting beside James looked over to his plate, which was already piled up with food, and grinned at him. James glanced over his shoulder to see who was looking, and saw a boy around his age, with black eyes, blond hair and light brown skin.

James asked, "What's your name? I'm James."

"I'm Peter," the other boy said. "Which room are you? I'm in room four, and I have desert powers."

"I'm in room two," James replied. Peter looked amazed.

"In room two? Who are your parents?"

"My dad is the commander of an underwater people named the Fesittes," James said.

"Then you've got water powers," Peter said. "You must be very powerful! Desert powers only consist of summoning sandstorms, controlling sand, speaking to desert animals and stuff. You can control water, shoot around in it, breathe and talk underwater, see in the water and you won't be crushed by the pressure!"

"Wow!" James exclaimed, amazed by his own powers, which caused several children to look in his direction.

After forty-five minutes, Cordova stood up again.

"Well, I hope everyone has enjoyed the meal. Now, we shall all head back to our rooms or take a walk around our base. The food will disappear in a few seconds." He snapped his fingers, and the food and drinks disappeared.

"Wow," James whispered. "How does he do that?"

"He snaps his fingers just as the servants take the food away," Peter responded. "Why do you ask so many questions? I think it's quite obvious."

James decided to change the subject.

"Okay, so as we aren't in the same room, let's take a walk around the base. Could you show me around?"

"Sure." Then, they joined the stream of people proceeding out of the hall. As they were going out, James noticed some badges that the children and Peter were wearing on their chest.

"What's that?" James asked.

"The badge? It's about seniority and skill. The numbers are for how many months you've been here, and the more skilful you are, the darker the badge is. You'll find one in your sack, but the number is zero and the badge is probably white."

Peter and James walked toward a huge, black building lit by dim lanterns. The words MAZE ARENA were painted between two lanterns that were brighter than the rest.

"That is a maze," Peter explained. "Every two months, all the children and teenagers go in there, and we are given full armour and weapons of our choice. The odd numbered rooms, one, three, five, seven, nine, eleven, thirteen, fifteen, seventeen and nineteen are one team, and the other rooms another. The most skilful person in a room will be the leader of it. The second and third will each take half of the room. In each room there are roughly ten or eleven people."

"But with so many people, how can they all fit?"

"There are loads of platforms, and even a second floor," Peter said. "There are also secret rooms, and if you happen to come across one there are chests with stronger or sharper weapons and armour. I normally take a bow and a quiver of arrows in there, because I'm not that good at swordplay." James spotted two dark figures opening the double doors out of the arena. They were holding what looked like knives, which he wasn't happy about, and they also started to head toward a patch of long grass.

"Who's that?" James asked, pointing toward the figures, but as Peter turned his head they had already vanished.

"What?" Peter asked.

"Nothing," James hastily said, but he was sure that he saw them.

"What do you mean?" Peter asked.

"I saw some people, figures, maybe demons. They probably hid in the grass over there."

"Maybe," Peter said anxiously, "but if they're demons, how did they sneak in? Maybe you were just seeing things. Let's just ignore it."

"No," James uttered. "I'll go there and find out what that's about. You can stay back here, but I'll go."

"I'll go with you," Peter said nervously. "But I hope they don't notice us."

James led Peter toward the long grass, but before entering it he skirted a bit to the right, belly crawled to the end of a tree trunk and peered around it. The two figures were also crawling, but they were making more noise. Soon, James could make out where they were. Making the least sound possible, he rolled behind a bush, and motioned Peter to follow. When he caught up with James, he put his ear against James's ear and whispered, "Should we go further around? It seems to be safer." However, he whispered too loud, and the two figures stopped moving.

James and Peter froze and ducked under the bush. For a while, the figures were silent. Then, as they started moving again, James said in the faintest whisper, "Now see what you've done! They suspect there's someone following them, and now we need to go in a larger circle, which will take more time." Peter was a bit angry, but he didn't say anything. James got onto his hands and knees and moved a few metres to his right, into some long grass. Then, he started walking, but with his back bent. When there was no more long grass ahead of him, he used his feet to propel himself swiftly behind a tree. He glanced around it and saw that the figures had stopped in front of a tree wider than the rest. James signed for Peter to follow again and continued on a route parallel to where the figures had moved, but he moved more rapidly. Finally, James and Peter were level with the huge tree, and the forms hadn't moved yet. James chose to go further into the jungle and turn back. Now, this deep in the forest, he could hear some birds and even some water. James and Peter belly crawled seven more metres, and when they turned around, the figures had vanished.

"Where could they have gone?"" Peter asked. "If there wasn't a secret passage down the tree?"

"There might be," James said. "Maybe I should tell Cordova."

"Yeah," said Peter, "let's go." They set off toward General Cordova's office, at the far end of the base. When they found his cabin and knocked on his door, there was no response.

"Where's he gone?" asked James. "Maybe he went out to do something."

"Maybe," Peter said nervously, "but I don't understand why he went. He hardly ever goes out."

"Perhaps this is one of the rare times that he goes out."

"But I'm still worried," Peter said. "He can't be-"

"Of course he can't be kidnapped," James interrupted. "This place's defence systems must be really good! I can't imagine these thugs sneaking in."

"You don't know," Peter whispered. "There are some secret passageways out of the base, but the entrances are so hidden, they are almost invisible."

"Really? Then how come no one creeps out of here?"

"We used to," Peter answered, "but then, seven months back Cordova banned it, and said that people who sneak out will be banished from the base. No one dared do it then, but I still try sometimes."

"With that risk?" James questioned. "You might be banished?"

"Yes," Peter said, "I like to do it, and so do a couple of my roommates. So, I keep doing it when I have the chance and no one's around."

"Wait," said James, "I think there's someone behind us." They spun around to see that Cordova had returned.

"There were two figures in the woods beside the maze arena," blurted out James. "They were holding knives, and they disappeared down a tree! Maybe they were demons."

"Boys, calm down first. Did you see their faces, or were they wearing masks?"

"They were too far away, and it was also too dark to see their faces," Peter said. "Where were you, anyway?"

"I was at the base of the alliance, Alatus. James, our base is formed by an alliance between different human species with their own powers, including the Fesittes. I was there to discuss our plans for the next Veltrion competition."

James looked surprised. "What's that about, and how do you do it? Is it our base against that Alatus base, or what?"

"No. Both bases chose a champion, and these two champions duel with their weapons of choice. First, we have room battles. The winners of each room will enter the maze arena and have a base battle. Then the winner of the battle will be the champion, who will fight in our arena."

"Then how do you become the champion? I mean, do we have to disarm or wound everyone else to be the winner, or the champion?"

"Each person will have a blue stone, set on the top of a pile of steep boulders. You have to prevent everyone else from getting your own stone to win. Of course, you could also get other peoples' stones."

"When is the competition?" James asked.

"The competition?" General Cordova said. "The room battles are on Friday. If you forgot, today is Wednesday."

"FRIDAY?" James blurted out. "We've got so little practice time!"

"I'm sorry, James," Cordova spoke, "but we cannot delay the competition. The Alatus base has already chosen their champion and is waiting for us." James looked sad and worried. "But don't worry," continued Cordova, "you already have superior fighting skills."

"Well, I'll just head back now. I need to make sure that I have some good training tomorrow." Next, James and Peter went through the winding corridors back to their rooms.

Six
His First Day

As it turned out, James would've had quite a good day of training if it wasn't for a few things. It all started when he was eating breakfast with Peter. There was a girl from his room called Alex, and she happened to be sitting opposite them. When they finished a delicious meal of bacon and sausages, General Cordova directed them off to their lessons. Rooms one, two, three and four would be having wrestling and boxing lessons first. As they walked down the path to the unarmed combat field, Alex muttered to James, "So you're the new kid, huh?"

Her friend, Carla, who was walking beside her, snickered in an annoying way. James and Peter decided to ignore them. Alex and Carla kept close to James all the way to the combat field, but fortunately they were organised in a different group. As James and Peter were practising punches, kicks, and wrestling, Alex constantly glanced at them to see what they were doing. Finally, the instructor told all of them to gather up around him, and that everyone was to partner up and fight each other.

"No hurting anyone," he said. "However, if you are hurt, cry out and we will bring you to the camp hospital." While he was saying this, a tall boy with brown hair and a mischievous look on his face made his way towards James. Following him was a black-haired boy, slightly shorter than the first boy, talking to him.

"Lukas, you must defeat him. We can't have him as the champion; he is so young and new."

"Maybe, but Ryan, even if I beat him up it is nearly impossible to become champion. There are much better boys here, and I cannot promise you I'll win."

So, there were two boys planning to become the champion. And the person who they didn't trust sounded like James, unless there were people who were newer than him. Then everyone spread out to practise unarmed combat, but Lukas and Ryan kept nosing around James and Peter.

"Hey," said James, "why are you walking around us?"

"Oh, we can't stay?" said Lukas stupidly. "It wasn't on the news." James doubted that there was even news on this remote location.

"Ignore them," said Peter in a low voice. So, James and Peter trudged off toward a corner of the field, but Lukas and Ryan chose the space beside them. They were talking to each other about James and snickering, as he tried to focus. Finally, the session was over. A boy named Carson got a scratch on his face, but otherwise everyone was okay.

Next, rooms two, four, six and eight went to sprinting class, and fortunately Lukas and Ryan were in room three. The instructor told everyone to stand in a horizontal line on the starting point. The finish line was a hundred and twenty metres away, and as everyone lined up, he called: "Go when I blow my whistle, start running as fast as you can towards the finish line. When you have arrived, you can either run or walk back here." What's a whistle, James thought, but he didn't say it aloud. The instructor waited until everyone was ready and blew the whistle. Of course, James could run fast, but there was a thin, black-haired boy who raced like a cheetah past everyone.

After the first race, James asked the boy, "What's your name?"

The boy smiled. "I'm Oliver," he said. "You're the new kid, right?"

"Yeah. Do you have any transportation powers to help you run so fast?" But then the instructor came over and talked about how you should run and the correct starting position, and Oliver decided to return to his own spot.

After both sessions, there was lunch at the dining pergola. Lukas and Ryan spent the whole hour talking to each other and staring at everyone, but General Cordova was not looking in their direction. However, James and Peter ignored them and tried to eat a peaceful meal. After lunch clouds started to cover the sky above, and the temperature began to drop, but everyone was still having lessons. Rooms one, two, three and four would be taking archery lessons, and on the way to the archery arena the rain started to pour. At first it was just a drizzle, but it grew until water was pounding against the corridors all over the base. Now, all the kids were streaming towards the field, and James discovered that it wasn't roofed. The instructors organised everyone into two rows, gave them a bow and three arrows and told the first row to shoot at the targets. James's vision was blurry through the rain, but Peter's arrow hit the edge of the bullseye. After the first shot, they nocked another arrow on the bowstring and fired. James glanced at the other children after the second shot. Carla's shot was close to the centre of the bullseye, but Alex's arrow stood quivering at the edge of the target. After the third shot, the second row took over the first row, and James and Peter got a rest.

"You're good," James told Peter. "Compared to me and some other kids." Indeed, most others' shots were wild. Peter looked disappointed.

"I could've done better, if it wasn't raining. But this might continue. Maybe there's a whole hurricane coming this way, and most of the training areas are outdoors," he sighed. "If only there was a place with a waterproof roof for everything." James looked around. Most of the other kids were neither chatting nor walking around. He thought that they were bothered by the downpour and the cold temperature.

Then, the instructor barked, "First group, come and replace the second group," and the first row made their way to the front. This time, the children's aim was little better. Of course, Peter and Carla's shots were fantastic, but James's arrows stood at the edge of the target. When the session finished, everyone's wet clothes were weighing them down, and they trudged down the corridors which thankfully weren't leaking toward one of the arenas to practise swordplay.

The sword arena had a retractable roof that could fold and unfold, similar to the colosseum's. The instructor allowed them to rest and change into armour at one side. After a few minutes everyone was ready, and the session began. The instructor first started teaching everyone the basics, but then more advanced parries and strikes. One of them was a difficult manoeuvre that included having to lurch your sword to the right, swiftly step to your left and strike at the right, and few people managed to do it correctly. After forty minutes of training, James was among the only people who could correctly manage all the moves that were taught. Finally, the children were asked to find a partner and duel.

"Well-" Peter began, but Lukas came over and interrupted him. "Yo, new boy, you see them doing all the good moves there? I bet you can't do that."

James was annoyed: "I'll show you what I could do after a while."

Lukas laughed: "After a while? I suppose you've got to practise it?"

James was so angry that he lost control and attacked Lukas by sidestepping and swinging his sword in an overarm strike, but Lukas was too fast, and he parried the blade. Lukas attempted to counterattack by slashing at James's legs, but he jumped upward and drove his blade down at Lukas's shoulder. He just managed to jump back and deflect James's sword. James lost balance and stumbled backward a few steps.

A moment later, the instructor walked over to them and asked, "Is there anything wrong?"

Lukas hastily said, "No, instructor. I'm just seeing how James can improve and teaching him tricks."

But the instructor frowned. "I've watched you for a while, and you and James seemed to be duelling. But not friendly, instead you seemed to be trying to injure each other."

"James started it, sir. He attacked me first."

"No," James cut in, "he was annoying me and laughing at me."

"You both go to your partners and practise!" the instructor shouted. Lukas went back to where Ryan was practising his more difficult moves. James kept practising and teaching Peter until the end of the session, when they had free time in their rooms until dinner.

When the session finished, everyone filed out to find that the rain had not stopped. They quickly walked up the corridors towards their rooms. James went to room two, and Peter went to room four, but they were close and could've been able to see each other through the windows if room three wasn't there. When he arrived, James immediately headed to his sleeping bag. After tidying up his belongings, he listened to the others chatting with each other, but the rain pounding on the roof made the talking hard to hear. James wished that Peter was also in room two, so he would have someone to talk to. He lay down on his sleeping bag and rested for half an hour until dinner.

Over the half an hour the rain had gradually become smaller, until it was no more than a light drizzle at sunset, but the fierce winds were still blowing. Lukas and Ryan were also annoying everyone at dinner. They constantly walked around to see what everyone was eating, muttering to each other, but most people ignored them. General Cordova was present, but you were allowed to walk around the dining pergola, so he didn't mind. James looked at Alex and Carla, who were at the other end of the table. The table was so long that he could barely hear them, but they were talking about demon attacks. He didn't know how they knew about that, but something suddenly came to him.

"Peter," James asked, "who rules the demons? Did he ever attack this base?" Peter looked up from his plate.

He said, "Their emperor, Gremword is at the centre of the huge forest in the Kingdom of Alemis-"

"Alemis," James said suddenly. "I've heard that before, but I'm not sure where."

"Really?" Peter said. "That's, well, I was saying, Alemis is around fifteen hundred kilometres away. The only way there is by sea, unless you want to build a bridge or dig there. His main palace is surrounded by volcanoes, trenches, tunnels, defence systems, smaller bases and gigantic armies of demons. He used to look like a demon, but in the last assault on them by our alliances someone sprayed a potion on the ground, and somehow the potion stayed there until Gremword came out in battle. He stepped on it, and the potion made his head hurt or something, then, somehow, he turned into a snake. He's been recovering for seventeen years, but some say that he's already strong and planning an attack on us and every tribe in the alliance."

"So why doesn't someone just attack him?" questioned James.

"No one dares to do that," said Peter. "The huge forest is full of traps, underground hideouts and wild animals. And if Gremword has recovered, he would make flash floods, hurricanes and winds so strong that trees could be uprooted into the intruders' paths."

After dinner, they were still allowed to walk around the base, so Peter and James went for a walk again. The rain had stopped, and there were only puddles and pools of water both on the corridors and on the grass. As soon as they crossed to the nearest corridor, James asked, "Can you show me other buildings around the base?"

Peter nodded. "Sure. There's a circuit for horse riding, and other buildings for meetings and stuff. There's also a climbing wall and a sand pit for jumping, but my favourite lesson is hunting class. Once in a while they will lead us onto the mountains around the base and let us hunt wild animals. They aren't too dangerous here, there are no demons, but tigers and wolves do live there. 'Have some real experience on this,' they say, when someone asks why they don't just teach us the stuff in the base. But before all that I would like to show you the fountain behind the rooms. It is magnificent, and it creates such a long rainbow." They strolled down the path leading to the rooms but walked into the bushes and undergrowth after a few metres. "There's a clearing," Peter whispered. A minute later, they arrived at the fountain. Around it were patches of colourful flowers, and spruce trees. "Watch this," Peter said. He took out a small packet from his pocket. As he opened it, fresh mist poured out of it and created a rainbow stretching from one end of the clearing to another. "This bag sucks a lot of moisture into it, but it can also let the mist come out," Peter explained. "I have a few more of these in my bag with my toiletries. It serves no real purpose, it's just fun to use."

After they got onto the path again, Peter led James to the climbing wall. It was made of real rock, and as steep as one of the cliffs surrounding the jungle. There were plants, boulders and puddles of water on the wall, Peter told him, but it could also shake violently. It was surrounded by low, iron walls, which were covered with dust and some mud from the wall. "I think we've got a climbing session tomorrow," Peter said.

"I'm not too bad at that." James stared at the climbing wall, or the cliff. There was no way that he would be able to climb up the steep wall, he thought. He didn't see many footholds or handholds, and the water on the wall glistened in the moonlight. "I think...That would be difficult to climb," James murmured.

"You'll be alright," Peter confronted him. "You just need practice."

"Okay," said James. "So where is the horse racing circuit?"

"It's down there," Peter replied. "I'll take you." They strolled toward the horse racing circuit.

They saw the moonlight reflecting from the iron fences before the actual track, the stands and the stables. The circuit was in an oval shape and was floored with sand and paint. There were the words STARTING POINT and FINISH LINE a metre apart at the stands. Other signs marked the 100-metre line, the 200-metre line and the 300-metre line. Above the finish line was the number of laps each horse had done. The stands were covered with hundreds of red seats, with three lines of stairs starting from the ground and leading to the seats. The stands had metal fences preventing anyone from falling out, and some of the fences had leaves or vines stuck on them. Beside the stands were the stables. There were twenty of them, in a row, and each one housed a horse. James could make out the forms of staff members pouring water and oatmeal for the horses and bringing stacks of hay.

"In the horse-riding session, we take turns riding and racing the horses around the circuit. There are four groups, and four stages. If you're good, then you're group one, if you're bad you are group four and if you're in the middle then you're group two or three. I'm in group three. Sadly, you always start at group four."

James looked at the horses. All of them were black or brown, except for one. It was a white stallion with tiny grey dots sprinkled around its body. There was a red triangle on its forehead. Then James noticed something above the horse's stable. It was dots, no, not dots. They were bodies of tiny creatures, crawling around. As he watched, more creatures came out and began dropping down to the ground. James didn't feel comfortable with the creatures, which looked like spiders. After a few minutes, he told Peter that he would be heading back to his room.

Seven
The Contest

The next day at breakfast, Cordova announced that there would be no sessions the whole day except for the room battles, as there were room battles for choosing the champion. The battles would take a lot of time, so Cordova decided to have three rooms battle together in one arena. Rooms one, two and three would fight in the sword arena, while four, five and six fought in the unarmed combat field. Then, the other rooms would fight, and rooms nineteen and twenty would fight at the end. After eating a supply of toast and butter the first six rooms went off to fight. As James said goodbye to Peter, he followed the other children heading towards the sword arena at once.

When they entered the sword arena, everyone gasped. Instead of the boring plain floor of stone, there was a river with a bridge over it. On both banks of the river were grass, and a lot of barrels, boulders and plants. There were ladders ascending to platforms on the wall, and holes in the ground to avoid. And there were piles of boulders scattered around. At the end of the sword arena, sitting on a chair on a high platform on the wall, was the instructor.

"Welcome," he said loudly so everyone could hear him, "to the room battles for the Veltrion competition. You may choose your preferred weapons, which are on the tables below me, but if it's a pole weapon or a bow you may only choose one. If it is a sword or a dagger, then you may select two. Everyone can have an extra shield!

Prevent anyone from taking your blue rocks and take theirs to win! If your stone is taken, you will immediately return here, and you are out of the battle. But if you don't return immediately, there will be consequences for you. You will fight until there is a winner, and the battle will start at the blow of my whistle." Then, all the children bolted for the weapons, so James followed. The table was made of smooth oak wood and stacked with weapons. There were bows, quarterstaffs, mace and chains, swords, daggers, shields, and about every other weapon. James selected a spear axe and a light, strong shield, and dashed toward his rock. He arrived just in time for the start of the battle.

Looking at all the other competitors, James decided not to attack too much, but rather to defend. His flag had three boulders facing the bridge, acting like a wall. He glanced around, taking in the sight. Already, two people were duelling on the bridge. Then he caught sight of Lukas. He wielded two short but sharp swords and a shield on his left arm, and he was coming straight for James's rock. James waited for him to come, but kept glancing at other people, and, luckily, they weren't coming for him. Then Lukas took him by surprise, screaming and leaping out of the boulders. James had barely turned when Lukas's shield slammed into his, sending them both sprawling. James got up swiftly, and swung his spear axe in a wide arc, aiming for Lukas's head, but Lukas was too fast. He deflected it with one sword and slashed at James's face with the other. Although James dodged, his hesitation bought Lukas some time. He feinted at James's stomach, sidestepped and stabbed at his back, only to be deflected by James's weapon, but he didn't see Lukas's other blade, which successfully drew blood from James's side. But James's next move defeated Lukas. He slammed his spear axe into the ground, narrowly missing Lukas's feet, and the force of it propelled James into the air, along with his spear. Lukas threw a sword, but James deflected it onto Lukas's other sword, leaving him weaponless. Then James came down with three slashes and a thrust, and that made Lukas's leg buckle under him. James kicked Lukas and sent him rolling away.

Then James turned just in time to see Ryan stepping out from behind a tree. He was armed with a spear and a shield, and as he ran toward James he roared, "How dare you do that to Lukas? I'll make you pay!" James stuck his spear axe in the ground and easily deflected Ryan's spear. Then, James spun around with his weapon, and Ryan leapt at James with his shield, but as fast as sound, he slid out of the way, causing Ryan to slam into the ground. But then, Lukas regained his consciousness and charged James. Although he parried his first strike, Lukas then feinted at his head and slashed at James's legs. James jumped, then Lukas punched him, and James fell to the ground. Lukas was about to remove James's stone when an arrow flew in their direction and hit Lukas's hand. He bellowed in pain, dropping James's stone back onto the boulders, and raised both of his swords, one of his hands dripping blood. Lukas was about to stab James when James rolled out of the way and kicked Lukas in the face. While Lukas staggered back, James got up and his blade almost hit Lukas's arm when something crashed into him from behind. James fell to the ground, and when he looked up both Ryan and Lukas were standing over him.

"Well," Lukas said, "I'll take the stone."

"No!" Ryan suddenly said. "I have the better claim-" James hit Ryan's back with the shaft of his spear axe and opened two rapid cuts on his thigh.

Then, James kicked into the air, but Lukas threw one of his swords. James deflected the flying weapon, and landed on Lukas's shield, but Lukas raised his remaining sword and tried to stab James. Then Ryan rose and used his spear to shove James off Lukas, only to be knocked once more to the ground by James. Then three arrows soared in their direction. Each arrow was aimed for one of them. One caught Ryan in the arm, one was deflected by Lukas's sword and one stuck on James's shield. James glanced at the direction the arrows came from. There was a pile of boulders beside the bridge, and an arrow sticking out of the gap between two rocks. The arrow was aimed straight at James. Just as the arrow flew, James used his spear axe to shove Lukas into its path, and the arrow caught him on his shoulder. Yelling in agony, he shook it off and used both of his swords to attack James from two directions. Ryan also hurled his spear at James. Seeing the blades, James ducked one of Lukas's swords and parried another, but he didn't see Ryan's spear. It was aimed for James's head, but instead it grazed his side, and blood ran down from the wound. Then Lukas kicked

James, and he rolled to Ryan's feet. Ryan was about to take away James's stone when Lukas tackled him.

"You!" Lukas screamed. "Leave the stone for me!" He picked up the stone when James grabbed his ankles and caused him to fall. Then, two more arrows flew over, hitting the stone and making Lukas drop it. Then, Ryan knocked Lukas's swords off his hands and threw them away. He kicked Lukas towards a tree, where he lay motionless.

Seeing that Lukas was out cold, James attacked Ryan. He deflected James's first swipe off his shield, but then James feinted at his head. Ryan raised his spear, and James slashed at his legs. Ryan cried out and rolled away. Then, James replaced his stone onto his boulders, but three arrows flew in his direction. One hit the stone, and the two others hit the shaft of his spear axe, just as Ryan's eyes opened, and he lunged at James with his spear. Although James deflected it, Ryan threw his shield.

It hit James's shield with amazing force and knocked him off balance. James only managed to steady himself with his weapon when Ryan hurled his spear. The missile buried itself in James's shield, but the force toppled him to the ground. Ryan laughed, but James was not wounded. He grabbed Ryan's spear shaft, kicked him and sent him sprawling. James got up to his feet, disarmed him and punched him, knocking him unconscious. With both of them stunned, James rolled them into a pile and looked out for more attackers. Sure enough, there were.

James glimpsed an archer and someone with two daggers fighting. Someone else was running toward him, wielding a double-bladed axe and a shield. Two others were duelling eight metres away with swords and a quarterstaff. He decided to deal with the axe-wielder first. His name was Jack, although James didn't know that. Jack ran for James, swinging his axe in wide circles, sensing that a victory was close. James ran up to meet the challenge. The duel started with James crashing his spear on Jack's axe. They fought for twenty minutes, and still neither of the two were hurt. Then, James made the mistake of trying to hit Jack on his head. He grabbed the shaft and used his axe to throw James to the ground. It must've taken a lot of his energy too, because he leaned on James's boulders for a few seconds before taking the stone back to his boulders. James was exhausted, but he returned to the table that used to hold the weapons. A lot of people were there, but somehow no one had found Lukas's and Ryan's stones undefended. James hoped that they would soon.

At lunch when the battles were over, James told Peter about his fight in the sword arena with Lukas and Ryan. Peter also told James about the story of how he picked off the other people before they were even close to him. When James was talking about the archer who was shooting arrows at them, Peter admitted that it was strange.

"You said that there was a pile of boulders," he began, "and the archer didn't show themself, but you also didn't see them. It's strange that they didn't show themself, not even to repel attacks, if there were."

"It might've been the archer fighting the person with two daggers," James pointed out. "He was quite close to the boulders." Peter thought about it.

"Yeah, but that archer might've gone there to get the other guy's rocks."

"Or the other way around."

"Fine," Peter sighed. "That must've been the case." Then he turned away from James.

After a fine meal of steak and pasta, the people who had fought in the morning walked to the archery field. When they arrived, they found that the targets had been removed; instead, there were six raised platforms. Sitting on a chair and in front of a table, was the instructor for the sword classes, who smiled when he saw them.

"Hello everyone," the instructor said loudly so everyone could hear. "I am the instructor for the sword classes, the swordmaster. I have heard that you have all done well in the room battles." Many children nodded their heads. "But, in each room there will be a champion, whose stone was either never taken or last taken. I will start with room one." No one moved. Everyone's eyes were fixed on the instructor, listening anxiously and carefully. "The champion is... Jack!" Jack's eyes widened in surprise and joy, and as he walked up to the platforms his friends clapped him on his back. After placing a black medal with the words ROOM ONE in gold on his shirt, the instructor put his hand on Jack's shoulder and said to him, "You've done well, Jack. Your stone was never taken away from your boulders, not even for a few seconds. But now, I must turn to room two." He turned towards room two and called, "In a few seconds, I will announce the champion of room two. And she is..." Everyone was silent, listening. "Alex!" James was taken aback by surprise. Surely there were people who were better than Alex? Then something annoyed him even more. Alex and Carla must've fought together, like Lukas and Ryan did. And Peter was not in his room, so he had no one to fight together with.

After all six champions were announced, they had free time in their rooms. After they had trudged along the corridors back to their rooms, James went to Peter's room to try calling him out, but Peter was also depressed from not being his room's champion. Instead, it had been a tall girl who James didn't know.

"It's so unfair," Peter complained. "She wasn't even good, and the instructor only picked her because he liked her."

"Yeah, I know how you feel, like, no one even found Jack's stone or bothered about stealing it for, like, twenty minutes, when he was fighting me. Who knew he would be that good?" Peter glared at James and left without another word.

That evening at dinner, Peter ignored James the whole time. James kept trying to talk to Peter, but Peter looked away every time. Finally, James gave up and ate his meal in silence. After dinner, Peter left straight for his room, but James wanted to explore all the other places in the base. After James had walked to a place where nobody else could see him, he left the corridor and entered the lawn, which was dotted with bushes and flowers. In nature, everything seemed so peaceful, everything so harmless, with nothing to worry abou-... thump! James tripped on something and fell into a bush. When he sat up, he realised that what he'd tripped on wasn't any old lump sticking out of the ground - it was a trapdoor, one camouflaged with grass and moss! Cautiously and curiously, James opened it. The creaking sound of it proved that it was very old, but even with risks that it might be a trap, James put one foot inside. Nothing curled around it, much less dragged him into the hole's dark depths. He put another foot in. Still nothing. Now, confident that nothing was down there, James let go and slipped inside. The hole was actually not very deep, but James's eyes could only see the corridor that he came from. Slowly, he crawled one metre, two metres. Then he realised that the tunnel was much longer than a few metres. It might be very long, even stretching out of the base. After crawling a few metres, James was afraid that he might get lost in the darkness. So instead, he climbed back up the hole, and headed for his room to sleep, wondering excitedly about what and where the tunnel led.

Eight
An Earthquake and a Dream

The next few days passed without any main events. On Monday, General Cordova announced that the battles between the champions of the rooms, the base battles, would be coming up on Friday, on the week after next week. On Saturday morning, James told Peter about the hidden trapdoor he'd found on Friday night, and Peter explained that it was a way out of school that they had found.

"Even the instructors don't know why it's there," Peter said.

"Then how did it appear there?" James asked. Peter didn't respond to that question.

It was on the Saturday of the next week that they felt the tremor. The ground shook, and everyone stopped what they were doing. James was having archery at the time. The arrows fell from the targets, then the targets collapsed onto the ground, flattening the arrows.

"Stay clear of any falling objects!" the instructor called. Everyone was running around in a panic, trying to avoid being crushed under the collapsing columns and roofs of the corridors. The screams of children mingled with the crashing of plummeting walls.

James and Peter stayed close to the centre of the field, and James yelled over the noise, "What happened?"

"No idea!" Peter said. "Must be an earthquake! There has been no such earthquake in this base before, though. This is strange." The tremor lasted for twenty minutes. By that time, no one thought it was an earthquake anymore. Most earthquakes only last for a few seconds, the longest one lasting for ten minutes. It was impossible for this tremor to be caused by nature, more likely to be a powerful creature or person, and no one knew anyone as powerful as that, except for...

"Gremword," Peter said. "But we'd know if he'd already recovered, right?" James asked.

"We might," Peter said. "But he could still conceal things from us. We don't know everything." James conceded the point. If Gremword was back, he thought, then surely he would launch an attack on this base or the Alatus base sooner or later? He would lead his army to destroy all of us, and then he would rule both Alemis and us. If that was it, then he had to be stopped by someone. James ate his dinner in silence. This time, he went straight back to sleep after dinner, as he was anxious to get rest.

That night, James had a dream. It started in a dense forest, where little sunlight managed to filter through the canopy above. A white house stood in the middle of a clearing beside a roaring waterfall, with extinguished campfires lying around it. Then, a black SUV swerved into the clearing. Peter had taught James over the past week about what modern people do and what technology they had, so James was able to recognise it as a car. As the SUV skidded to a stop, two humanlike figures opened its doors and stepped out.

One said, "You see, Hans, cars work much better than that slow, inefficient machine of yours." The person who just spoke was wearing a bulletproof vest, a black shirt and camouflage pants.

"I think not," the other said angrily. He was wearing a suit and a brown, wide-brimmed hat. "Mine cuts down trees and makes paths, while your car needs to plough through them!" The two made their way toward the house.

As the person with the camouflaged pants opened the mahogany doors, a voice from inside the house called, "Well, I see you have come, Hans. Did you bring the weapons?"

"Of course," the man called Hans said, but James couldn't see any weapon. "I'll show you." Then the dream changed.

In this dream, James was standing in a white house with a wooden door, which was open, but no one seemed to be able to see him. Someone wearing a silver suit stood in front of it, and two other people were entering the house. James realised that it was the same house that he'd seen in his first dream.

As the visitors sat down, the man wearing the silver suit ordered, "Bring out the weapons, Hans."

Hans pulled out two glittering, silver knives decorated with diamonds and jewels from his pocket, and said, "You see, Derek, you didn't need to worry about this being stolen. I am your most valuable man, unlike Nolan. He just drives the car."

"I did all the work," Nolan grumbled, but Hans and Derek ignored him.

"Well, but these knives are valuable. It might hold the

key to the destruction of all the people of the tribes in every alliance, including their children."

"Yes," Hans agreed, "but it is wiser to destroy their children first. If they survive, they will have their own kids and might regroup and form an army to defeat us. we can't risk that happening."

"But the only problem is finding the trapdoor and the tunnel, the only way inside the base-" James woke, and sat up in his sleeping bag, his forehead beaded with sweat.

The next morning at breakfast, James told Peter about his dream.

"Don't worry, it's just a dream," Peter comforted James. "It won't be real."

"But it seemed very real," James said.

"Do you know these peoples' names?" Peter asked.

"Well..." James thought for a few seconds. "One of them was called Hans, one called Nolan, and one called Derek," James said. "I heard them calling each other's names."

"Did you see what they were wearing?"

"Derek wore a silver suit, Hans a black suit, and Nolan a camouflage vest and a pair of army pants."

"I know them!" Peter suddenly said. "They're demons. I saw them in the first demonic war, passing by my desert village when I was five. They looked exactly like you described. But how did you dream about *them*? It's impossible for you to know about Hans, Nolan or Derek." Then he shook his head. "You might be lying, and you could've heard about them somewhere."

"I'm not lying," James insisted. "I did dream about Hans and Nolan." But this time Peter didn't respond. He didn't want to believe that James had that dream.

After breakfast, rooms two and four went down the corridors towards the edge of the complex. There was a door at the end of a corridor, and James figured that it would lead out of the walls of the complex. He was correct. When a teenager from room four opened the door, a small field lined with stables lay facing them. At the end of the field, which was around twenty metres long, was an iron gate. Standing beside the gate was the instructor of the hunting class.

"Hello, everyone," she said. (She was a woman, unlike the other instructors). "Welcome to hunting class. Please mount and saddle your horses, and if you need assistance, I will help you. Everyone went to saddle their horses, but James walked up to the instructor.

"Madam?" he asked. "This is my first hunting class, so, er, which horse do I get onto? Besides, I don't know how to saddle or ride a horse. Can you teach me?" The instructor studied him.

"Of course," she finally said, "I have a spare horse behind the stables. I'll lead it right here." Then she walked toward the stables, and came back in one minute, leading a brown Arabian horse back. "This will be your horse," she said, "that you will ride today. I'll show you how to control it." For the next ten minutes, James listened to his instructor talking about the correct way to saddle a horse and to ride it. Finally, everyone was ready, and the instructor had also saddled her own horse. The horses set off out of the complex.

First, the instructor led everyone into the forest. She explained that they were still within the borders of the base, but outside the complex.

"There are numerous animals in the island's forests," she said. "They run fast, but our horses are faster. There are several pockets on your horse's saddle, and some are filled with nets. You also have a knife in a scabbard tied to your horse's saddle. Graze the animal if you want to or slow it down. Trap it in your nets!" Then, groups of children and their horses began galloping off.

James wasn't sure what he should do, but Peter said, "Follow me. We split into groups when we hunt, because if too many of us are together the animals could sense us. I'd like you to be in my group today. And maybe we'll catch a few rabbits like you said. There's also a boy in my group called Leo. He's a room champion." Peter led James into the woods. After a while, they met with a group of people. There were three boys, all with dark hair, but one of them had hazel eyes while the other two had blue ones. There was also a girl riding on a white horse with dots on its head and jowls.

"Well?" one of the blue-eyed boys asked. "Can we begin now?"

"Yes," Peter said, and then whispered to James, "I'm the leader of this group." The group trotted into the woods.

After five minutes, James said, "There!" There had been a brown blur passing through the woods beside him. All around him, his groupmates galloped past him, yelling, throwing nets. James followed them for a few seconds, and then something happened. One of the boys slid off his saddle! James realised that the boy had thrown a net on the animal, which was a deer, but apparently the deer had pulled the boy off his horse. Now, the girl riding the white horse leapt down and grabbed hold of his leg, and the deer slowed down. James dismounted and quickly cut the deer on its leg, and the wound completely stopped it.

After tying the deer up, the group set off to find more prey. After another ten minutes of riding, they came to a loud river. But their horses could not leap over it, and there were no stones or fallen tree trunks to act as bridges, so they went parallel with the river. After another few minutes, they spotted two rabbits drinking water from the river in front of them, and they hadn't noticed the children. The green-eyed boy moved to the right side of the animals, while Peter advanced on them. Then suddenly, the rabbits turned. Seeing Peter, it jumped backward and knocked his friend into the river. Then it slowly walked backward and toppled into the water itself. Peter threw his net, but the animals were too far away. Everyone dismounted, and they waded into the river after the rabbits. Finally, one of James's groupmates threw a net, and trapped the rabbits. They stumbled back to their horses, tied the rabbits to Peter's horse, and rode away to find more prey. After a few minutes they came to a tree with a horde of birds. There were soon five birds hanging onto their horses. After that, they decided that they had got enough prey, so they headed back to the base.

Back at the stables, every other group had returned. Nets filled with small animals lay everywhere, and a dark-haired girl was talking to the instructor, saying, "My group hunted down two deer, but they were too big, so we tied them up."

James and Peter's group began placing the birds and rabbits that they had hunted on the ground, while Peter went up to the instructor and said, "We also brought down one of the deer. James wounded it, but it is not dead. We tied it up." The instructor was silent for a moment.

Then she called, "Everyone, you can rest for a minute. Then, I will announce the group who hunted the most animals, the winner of today's hunting class." All the groups went to their horses, unsaddled them, and led them to their stables. James led his horse to the back of the stables, and found a shaded, walled area there with hay lying around. James opened the gate and led his horse inside the area. Then, when he went back to his group, he found everyone standing in front of the stables. The instructor was saying, "The winning group today has hunted two deer, seven birds and even three fish. And that is...Alexandra's group!" The dark-haired girl that James had seen talking to the instructor stood up and smiled. Her group followed her as she walked toward the instructor. Peter scowled at her.

"She thinks she's so pretty," Peter muttered quietly. James didn't hear him. How did they hunt so much, he thought. After the end of the lesson, the children walked toward the dining pergola and had lunch.

A few days later, James had almost forgotten the tremor. It was at dinner next Wednesday that the storm hit them. Everyone was eating peacefully, and the hall was filled with chatting people when the storm cloud was seen. Occasional flashes of lightning mixed with the heavy rain in the distance, and they could feel the wind becoming more and more powerful. The children became silent, watching the storm draw nearer to their island. And in a few minutes the wind and the rain hit them. It was chaos. Plates and cutlery blew onto the floor, rain mixing with the water in their cups. Some people ran for their rooms, and some stayed inside the pergola. General Cordova remained calm, just holding his plates on his table and eating unhurriedly, despite all the noise. James and Peter ran to their rooms. The wind blew the rain inside the corridors, and lightning struck a nearby tree. At least the tunnel will probably be flooded, James thought. When they got in front of their rooms, Peter blew water from his mouth.

"How is Cordova always so CALM?!" he muttered.

"Don't ask me," James said. Soon, they were joined by several other people, standing in their rooms. It was a few minutes before the storm receded and the clouds floated away.

At breakfast the next morning, James felt suspicious about the storm and the tremor. It was almost like they were connected, like they both came from the same evil source of power. Even more, that night he had dreamt about the man in the black suit, Hans, and a few other humanlike men on a self-rowing boat. Hans was looking at the beautiful silver knives, but this time he didn't tell Peter. He wanted to keep it a secret. But what were they doing?

The next Friday, the whole base was excited to see the base battles. The champions from each room (Jack, Alex, Carson, Audrey, Logan, Marcus, Callum, Charles, Isaac, Daniel, Leo, Robert, Austin, Liliana, Adam, Maximillian, Alan, Oscar, Alison and Xander) were going to fight in the sword arena to decide which three children would be the champions of the base. Everyone swarmed to the arena and sat in the stands. The arena looked the same as James had seen in the room battles, a river, bridge, boulders, trees. Piles of rock lay everywhere, with coloured stones on top of them.

The instructor called loudly, "Champions, you know the rules! You will select your preferred weapons, and if your stones are stolen, then you are out of the competition. Take stones from others and protect your own, until there are only three stones left! Good luck!" And with that, the battle began.

Nine
A Plan

As soon as the whistle blew, James kept his eyes focused on Jack and Alex. He thought that Alex wouldn't attack other people, but she did. As she fought her way to Jack's stone with her gleaming steel swords, James was amazed by how well she hacked her way through. When Alex was almost to Jack, he suddenly turned and swung his double-bladed axe in two circles, but Alex wasn't waiting for him to stop. She bashed in straight with her shield, stopping Jack's axe. Then, she used one sword to knock off Jack's stone and used the other to ward Jack off. But when Alex grabbed hold of the stone, Jack leapt over Alex and slashed down in an overhead cut. At the last moment, Alex dodged the axe and knocked Jack with her shield. But then, two arrows flew in her direction, fired from a blonde-haired boy.

"That was Callum," Peter told James. One of the arrows hit Jack's stone, and one of them was sliced in half by Alex's sword. She picked up the sharp flint on the arrow and ran back holding Jack's stone. As they watched, he woke and stumbled back to the weapon racks.

Alex fought like a devil, wounding other competitors, and defending just as well. Even arrows couldn't get close to her, for those were sliced in half. Out of the corner of their eyes, James and Peter caught glimpses of other duels. As Callum shot Leo and Robert, Alan backed Isaac to the river. But behind her, Marcus was coming for Alex, and she didn't see him. As he pounced with his spear, Alex suddenly swung both of her swords upward, backflipped and kicked at Marcus's spear. Although her legs were deflected off Marcus's shield, he still fell to the ground and rolled back a metre. When Alex came down at him with her weapons, Marcus rolled out of the way and raised his spear. To avoid the missile, Alex staggered back, and in that split-second Marcus stood up and swiped his long, grey spear in a circle. Alex hurled her sword, but it was deflected by Marcus. James could see what was in Marcus's eyes. It wasn't anger, it was determination. Spear in his hand, he charged Alex when she wasn't paying attention, knocked her off balance, and reached out slowly for her stone...

Crash! The sound of Alex knocking down Marcus echoed around the arena. After seeing Marcus going down, Alex put back the stone and opened a cut in his chest. But Marcus's reflexes were also fast. As he rolled, he stood up again and swung his spear around to stab her, only to be parried by her blade. Now Alex attacked, however her two strikes were both dodged by Marcus. He feinted, ducked and propelled his spear at the direction of Alex's leg, and she couldn't sidestep in time. The sharp spearhead pierced her thigh, and as her blood gushed out Marcus took her stone. Alex slowly limped toward the tables, when the battle ended.

"Well!" The instructor shouted. "Now we have our winners: Marcus, Alex and Liliana!"

"Oh great," Peter muttered, "just what we need. Another girl who's on the champions list. What do we do now?" James didn't say anything. Although he didn't like the idea of too many girls being the champions, he also felt that it was rude.

"Well," the instructor called, "now that the base battle has finished, we may all go to lunch! But today's lunch is a feast, to honour our new champions! They have done well in battle and deserve our appreciation." Peter snorted. Do we actually need a feast to honour them, he thought.

At the dining pergola, the plain wooden tables were exchanged for beautifully decorated metal ones. Platters of food and bottles of drink lay around the tables, roast chicken, salads, pasta, soup. As the children gathered around the tables, smacking their lips, the three champions sat at the head table, along with the other competitors of the base battle. They enjoyed hours of feasting, celebrating and chatting, far into the afternoon, when at three o' clock Cordova announced that they would have a special lesson that day- for the children to learn how to master their powers and control them. The rooms one, two, three and four would be having the lesson in the unarmed combat field, and when they arrived the unarmed combat session's instructor was waiting for them.

"Welcome!" he said. "In this session I will teach you how to manage your powers. If you already know how to use your powers, please practise them, and I will come to each of you to improve your knowledge and control of your powers." The rest of them lined up. James followed them, and saw some people creating flames, or rocks out of thin air. One of them was concentrating on a rock, and as James watched the person made the rock float off the ground, but James wasn't sure what to do. Then the instructor came over to him.

"Hello, James," the instructor said gently. "I am here to teach you what powers you have, and how to use them. I believe that your father is a Fesitte, yes?"

"Uh…" James didn't really know much about his father. "I don't know."

"Then did you ever do anything special, that other people could not do, in your life?" James thought for a minute.

"I could fight pretty well."

"You are good at fighting, because you inherited that from your father, the commander of the Fesittes. But your father had a special power, which was controlling water. And his powers passed on to you."

"Okay. How do I perform my powers?" The instructor thought about how to explain it to James for a short time.

"First," he said," to lift water you must concentrate on the water that you want to lift. Then, you raise your hand slowly, and the water will rise." James looked around for a water source and saw a teenager lifting up a bucket with his eyes' powers. James concentrated on the bucket and raised his hand, but only one drop of water rose from the bucket.

"It doesn't work," James said.

"You need to practise," the instructor said. "Now you can practise it, while I assist some other children." After the instructor went away, James kept practising lifting water until he succeeded.

When he succeeded, James thought, now I can lift water. What about moving water sideways? James then practised concentrating on water and using his hand to slowly move it sideways, and then after a few times he managed it! Now he was ready to try something more difficult. He spotted some water lying on the ground, concentrated, moved his hand in a circular motion and the water ran around in circles. Then he made the water stop, and practised squeezing the water into different shapes, splitting it in half, and even giving it a ride in the air. Then James thought, if I could control water, and wood floats, then I could also carry wood into the air too! But when he tried, the wood suddenly dropped down and hit the ground, nearly hitting someone. Then the instructor appeared at his side.

"This can sometimes happen," he said. "You might even lose control of your powers when you are angry or scared, but don't worry if it doesn't go well. And this session has ended!" he called. "Goodbye, and you may all return to your rooms now." Then they all filed back to their rooms, to spend some free time before dinner. They had a regular dinner in the pergola after an hour, and they all headed back to sleep.

But James lay awake for many hours, thinking about the battle that day, but then about the demons and the trapdoor. Finally at midnight, he decided that he wanted to find out more about the trapdoor and its uses. He silently crept past towering pillars that cast ghastly shadows across the marble corridors, which seemed to consume grass and bushes. At last, he came to the point where he had remembered the trapdoor to be. He left the corridor and ran to the trapdoor, and opened it...

"What are you doing here, James?" asked Peter. James jumped at him saying that so suddenly, and when he looked around Peter was crouching in a bush behind him.

"What are you doing?" asked James.

"Well," Peter replied, "I decided to come for a walk because I couldn't sleep, and I found you, so I followed you. So, what are *you* doing?"

"Well..." James found himself blushing as he said that. "I wanted to look at the tunnel, because it's a way inside the base. Do you have anything that you want to share with me?"

"I, well," Peter's eyebrows suddenly furrowed together in concern. "I thought of General Cordova when I was walking, and I started looking for him, just for fun. But I couldn't find him anywhere, and he's usually outside at night. He sleeps really late."

James was really confused and didn't know what to say, and at that moment a voice behind them said, "Hello, James and Peter," which caused them both to jump.

"General Cordova!" shouted Peter. "Where have you been?"

"Well," Cordova said, "I have been at the Alatus base to inform them that we have already selected our champions, and to discuss the date of the final battle, between our champions and theirs."

"Then could you tell us the location of the Alatus base?"

Cordova thought for a while.

"The Alatus base is high in the sky, invisible to normal men," he said. "But if most men saw it, they could only fly a helicopter into it. But the Alatueans could fly, and that's how they got up there."

"Then how did *you* get up?"

"I called one of them down, with a pair of wings," he said. "Then I flew. Now that I have told you about me, what are you doing here?"

"Oh." Peter said, "I was taking a walk, but James somehow had the idea of descending into the tunnel-"

"NO!" James shouted. "I was just walking by, and Peter hid in the bushes and tried to scare me."

"Well," Cordova said, "why don't you go back to sleep?" For a moment, James and Peter were speechless.

Then Peter said, "Yes. We'll head to our rooms now." Then, they went back to their rooms and to sleep, but Cordova watched them for a minute before heading back to his own cabin.

That night, James had another dream, and this was about Hans, Nolan and a band of people wearing black shirts and jeans sailing on a small wooden self-moving boat. Hans was intently studying the knives, while Nolan asked him miserably, "When will you end this quest?"

"When we find it," Hans replied. He had tried to hide it, but Nolan saw the frustration in his voice.

He sat down on a bench, just as one of the others said, "Something new appeared on the map."

"Where?" Hans asked excitedly.

"Here," the man said, holding up his map. "A new mass of islands suddenly appeared."

"Oh great," Nolan grumbled, "more torture."

Completely ignoring Nolan, Hans stated, "It might be in there. Look for islands with forests."

"When will we find the freaking *island*?!" shouted Nolan.

Looking over, Hans said, "Oh, if we search all the islands, then probably two weeks. But they'll still be able to see us if we can't see them." Then James woke up with a start.

That morning, he went to tell Peter about his dream.

"You dreamed about Hans and Nolan *again*?" Peter exclaimed, surprised. "You already dreamed about them a few days ago!"

"I don't know how," James admitted. "It just happened."

"I mean, yeah," Peter said, "but it's strange that you've dreamed about people that you don't know again. It's almost like the dreams are real and that you could see things that it isn't possible for you to know in your dreams...I think we should tell Cordova."

"Sure," James replied. When they told Cordova about it, his eyebrows furrowed into a frown.

"These knives are tools that could be used to break into our base, and with these demons trying to use it, it proves to be a threat. It is also unusual that James could see these things that are happening, happened or would happen that it is impossible for him to see." Then he thought for a while. "The first dream was beside a waterfall, right? And the second dream was on the ocean. Plus, James has water powers. So, I believe that it is because of all this, that James has this power. We will have a meeting about Hans's threat after breakfast. But now, enjoy your breakfast!"

After breakfast, General Cordova announced that there would be a meeting in the number one meeting room, and that all the room champions and James and Peter would attend it. It started with James informing the rest of them about his dream, but they didn't believe him.

"It might be fake," Carson said. "After all, it's only a dream."

"Yeah," Alan and Robert agreed, "don't trust him."

As they were all turning away, Peter shouted angrily, "James dreamed about Hans and Nolan twice! It means that these two dreams are connected, and that James was NOT lying."

"But you're James's friend," Carson complained lazily, "you could be working together to tell us this lie." And then James got angry and lost control. Somehow, water sprouted from his palms, and without thinking, he blasted it onto Carson.

"Ugh!" Carson yelled. He was so angry that flames flickered across his body.

"Stop fighting!" Cordova shouted over the noise. "James did dream about Hans and Nolan, who are demons sailing in a ship, on a mission to find our base. We should prevent them from searching any further before they find our base or launch a quest to intercept them."

"I don't believe this."

"James is right," Cordova said. "He's seen demons holding beautifully decorated silver knives that I know are tools that could be used to break into our base."

"Fine," Carson said stupidly. "But I'm only listening because it's you who said it."

After that, most people agreed that they should launch a quest to intercept Hans, except for Peter.

"We should kill Gremword instead," he said. "If he's dead, then the demons will also be weakened. That way, we could do two things together! We would still need to murder Gremword, right?" James quickly agreed, and to his surprise so did Alex, Marcus and Liliana. But everyone else doubted that his idea would work.

"If you don't agree, then don't take part. The rest of you can sabotage Hans."

"Well, the decision is made!" exclaimed Cordova before they could say anything.

"But five of us against Gremword and his armies..." stuttered Marcus.

"We'll do fine," put in James. "General, could you provide enough provisions and strong horses for each of us? And a ship would be useful."

"Hmm," Cordova scratched his beard. "The food, water and horses we can manage. But I am afraid that we have no available ships, except for three smaller boats. You might not fit the horses on them."

"Hmmm." The champions considered the problem.

"Then once we reach Alemis, we'll walk to Gremword's palace," Marcus decided. They all looked at him. "Right?" he said. "Walking won't hurt us." Alex cleared her throat.

"Marcus," she said crossly. She was already angry at him for almost taking her stone away. "Horses are faster, and what if there are thorns and traps? At least with a horse, there is a chance that we won't die."

"Hmph," Marcus muttered. "Horses go faster. I suppose she'll run herself into a tree or something. Also, it's unfair to the horses-"

"IF YOU THINK YOU'RE SO SMART, THEN..." Alex screamed.

"Then what?" Marcus asked calmly in an annoying manner.

"FIGHT ME!" Alex yelled. "I WILL PULVERISE YOU!"

"Stop fighting!" Cordova's voice filled the room, even though he wasn't shouting. "Now, who wants to ride horses, even though they can't fit on the boat?" Alex's hand shot up, but she was the only one who agreed.

"WHAT???" Alex screamed at the top of her voice. "NO ONE'S SUPPORTING ME?"

"Yes," Marcus said, "Because it's you. Instead, everyone wants to support me." Alex stormed out of the room, slamming the door shut behind her.

"Well," Cordova said, "I believe that we have agreed on not bringing horses. Alex should stop being angry by tomorrow, and you six will set out on the boats to Alemis and the quest the day after tomorrow. The meeting is finished!"

The next day, the quest group began to prepare their belongings. James put a spare set of clothes, two water-skins, enough food for the journey, some bandages and his favourite sword from the sword arena in his bag. Unlike the other champions, he didn't include a tent, as that would just make his bag heavier. And then, they followed Cordova with their bags to the base's boats.

The boats weren't small. They weren't too big either. Each boat was the size of a small yacht, at the front were the driver and engine, and at the back were the sofas and beds. There was also a bottom layer, where they could store their belongings. Each boat could house three people, and then as Cordova taught Alex and Liliana (who were the chosen drivers) how to control the boats, James and Peter explored each vehicle's interior.

"I'll probably die of boredom before a demon kills me," Peter groaned. "There's nothing to do here." Indeed, they did not see any books or games.

"Wait," James said, "there's a hatch here."

"Hmm," Peter said, "open it." James opened the hatch, and there was a chest.

"Open that," Peter said. James opened the chest, and there were a few board games and three extremely thick books about exploring in it. "Okay," Peter said gloomily, "now at least we won't die of boredom. But it'll still hurt my brain very much."

After returning to the complex, the quest members tried to spend a peaceful last night full of rest. But James thought anxiously about the incoming quest for many hours, and when he finally fell asleep, he had another horrible dream. In his dream, he was hovering over the water over Hans and Nolan's boat, but they couldn't see him.

As he followed their boat, one of the sailors asked, "Should we search that island?" He pointed to an island with steep cliffs and thick forests, and for a few seconds James feared that it was theirs. But that island, unlike their base, was surrounded by other islands, so it couldn't be the base. Anyway, Hans agreed to search it, while Nolan grumbled unhappily about their mission. Then, as the enemy boat headed toward that island, something caught the sailor's eye. "Look!" he cried, but when he turned it was gone.

"What?" Hans asked.

"I saw it for a second," the sailor said nervously. "It was a flash of sunlight in the air. It could only have come from a piece of glass."

"Ignore it," Hans said quickly. "That couldn't harm us." Then James woke, but it was still the middle of the night. And something that he hadn't realised was that the flash of sunlight he'd seen was Leo's binoculars, and that their base was invisible to demons. But this time, he fell asleep quickly...and had another dream.

In his second dream that night, although James wasn't sure why, he dreamed of Hans and Nolan again. They were still on the boat, but this time the boat was almost on the shore of an island.

"Is that it?" Nolan complained.

"No," Hans replied. "We'll go ashore."

"Then I'll stay on board," Nolan said unhappily. "I hate this mission-"

"Sir!" a sailor suddenly said and pointed to the water. "There's a whale!" Sure enough, an orca was lurking a few metres away from the boat.

"Get away from the whale!" screamed Hans, but the orca prevented them from leaving with its fins.

"I'll help you get away from me," said a rumbling noise inside the sea. Then the orca splashed its fins and sent a massive wave towards the boat. All the demons flew into the air and landed in the water, and James woke up. This time it was morning.

Ten
To the Forest of Demons

At breakfast that day, the quest group said goodbye to the rest of the base. After a huge breakfast, James and Peter still felt hungry and listened to Cordova making his farewell speech. After a few minutes, the whole base's children gathered up at the top of the cliff and bid the champions farewell, though a few children had puzzled expressions on their faces. There were lots of goodbyes and farewells from the other children, but it all ceased when Cordova began to speak.

"Children," he began, "this may be an awkward time to make a speech, and although most of you already understand the meaning of this quest, I will inform the rest of you who don't know about it yet, that they are leaving to kill the Demon Lord, Gremword, who dwells at the heart of the treacherous Forest of Demons. There, he has plenty of soldiers, minions, generals, as it is a kingdom where the majority of demons live." Gasps were audible from the crowd of listening children. After a brisk pause, Cordova continued, "The reason for killing Gremword is that James has had dreams about Hans and Nolan, two of the evil Lord's minions, sailing a boat close to our base. They would locate us sooner or later, but after they have done so they would report back to Gremword, and then the demons will attack. However, if Gremword is killed, the assault will be meaningless, as there will be no leader to guide them. The journey will be difficult, crossing through hazardous, rough terrain, and they might encounter demons, but we must prevail, for the future of our camp is in their hands." Cordova finished, but looking at the worried faces in the crowd, he added, "Even though the demons are large in number, they are both unintelligent and inexperienced. Let us all wish James and his friends good luck!" He smiled, and saw many others beaming as well.

After General Cordova's speech, the quest group boarded their boats, but James went to Cordova and said, "General Cordova, can you organise an attacking force of our base's soldiers to invade the demons? We will kill Gremword, and it would probably make invading the demons easier. So…can you arrange the attacking force?"

Cordova thought about it for a moment, and said to James, "Yes. I suppose that we will be able to gather a large enough force to invade the Forest of Demons. Also, if you five manage to come to the beach of the forest, we will bring you back to this island." James hugged Cordova and said goodbye to him. While Alex and Liliana went to the front to start the boats, James and Peter went to the back and waved at the base's children one last time. Then, after a last glance at their base, the boats set off toward Alemis.

"This is boring," James said. It was the third day of their quest, and they still hadn't reached Alemis.

"Let's go see what Marcus is doing," Peter suggested. "It might be fun just to watch him for a while." They both walked to the side of their boat. James could see Alex driving. In their three days at sea, James and Peter had explored all the corners of the boat, and they still found no games except for the ones that they had found the day before the quest started. When they looked at Marcus and Liliana's boat, Marcus was on the top deck, looking at the horizon.

When he saw James and Peter, he called, "Hey! I see a landmass in front. Do you suspect that's part of Alemis?"

Peter looked in the direction he was pointing, and saw a piece of land in the distance, drawing closer.

"Could be," Peter replied. "We should be able to reach it before sunset."

"I can see smoke there," James observed. "What does that mean?"

"Probably one of the volcanoes that Gremword and the demons made," Peter said. "Let's go up to the top deck and look around and see if we can spot something."

When James and Peter arrived at the top deck, Marcus called, "Hey, I think there's a village! And there's a line of shining yellow stuff, maybe it's gold!" Peter handed James his binoculars. When James looked through it, he could see a village, and what looked like a golden highway. Cars sped on the highway, and when James looked to the horizon, the highway led to... An endlessly vast forest!

"Is that the Forest of Demons?" James asked, pointing to the forest.

Peter gasped, "It is!"

Marcus had also spotted the forest, and was now calling, "Look over there! Is that the Forest of Demons?"

"I see it!" Peter called back.

"I think it is!" James wanted to tell Alex to drive the boat toward the forest, but, before he could go to Alex, the boat steered in the direction of the Forest of Demons. Then, James and Peter went below deck, but Marcus still stayed on the top deck scanning the horizon.

Five hours later, the two boats arrived at the coast of Alemis, on the outskirts of the Forest of Demons.

When they had unloaded their packs, Liliana asked, "Do we keep our boats here?" Everyone froze. They had just realised that demons might steal their boats, and if that happened, they would not be able to get back to base.

"Just leave it here," James suggested. "Tie it up, cover it with branches and sand and maybe the demons will think it's a wreckage."

"Okay," Marcus said. "*Maybe.* Extremely reassuring." But James and the others still covered the boats up, and when they finally ventured into the forest it was already night time. "Aren't we supposed to sleep now?" Marcus asked.

"Let's sleep a bit later," James responded. "First, we explore the forest a bit, and make sure nothing will attack us while we sleep. We also need resources to make a bed."

"WHAT?" shouted Marcus. "We're well enough protected in a tent!"

"But there are insects that can kill you," Peter said. "We have to sleep on a raised platform, inside our tents."

"Fine," Marcus growled, "but I won't sleep on a raised platform. I won't waste time setting it up."

"Right," James said, "me and Peter will explore the area, while you three can set up camp here. Sleep if you want to." The rest of the group agreed.

"But remember to put stones around the place where you sleep!" Peter added. "Some dangerous bugs avoid stones." Then, James and Peter set off into the forest.

"No sign of any bears or tigers here," Peter said. "One hour, and we didn't find anything that could be a threat."

"Wait," James said. He'd just spotted some footprints on the ground. "Are these...tiger prints?" Peter also saw them.

"I think...it's a boar," he said.

"Should we follow it?" James asked.

"No," Peter replied, "that'll lead us further away from the camp. I suggest we go back now." Then James noticed that it had started to rain, and that the wind was beginning to blow stronger.

"Good idea," he said, "it's raining." When they arrived at their base, Liliana was still setting up her tent. Alex was sitting in front of her tent, looking at the horizon of the ocean. James looked around the area, and saw a tent fully set up, with the figure of Marcus inside in it.

"I'll make a fire," Peter said. Liliana came to them.

She successfully set up her tent, and asked, "Did you two find food?" James swallowed. He hadn't really thought about eating, and now when he thought of it, he realised how hungry he was. But then, he didn't see any animals in this part of the forest.

"Um..." James stuttered. "We didn't find...any animals, except for some footprints that belonged to a boar."

"Fine." The two girls walked back to their tents to sleep. James reluctantly began to set up his own tent, and at that moment Peter returned with a bunch of fallen tree branches and started rubbing them together to make a fire.

After setting up his tent, James told Peter, "I'll be the guard for the first three hours, and you sleep. Then after around three hours, I'll wake you up."

"Sure," Peter said. Then he went to sleep, while James sat down on the soft sand and scanned the forest for any sign of movement. There was nothing that might be a threat. Then he stared at the fireplace, and thought about the dangerous adventure ahead, that he might lose some of his friends. And the champions were also starting to become his friends. At two in the morning, Peter woke up and switched posts with James. But going to sleep gave him more dreams.

That night James dreamed about Hans and Nolan again. They and their group of sailors were boarding their boat, saying, "It's not on this island either. We need to search somewhere else." Nolan looked extremely grumpy, but this time he didn't say anything.

"But we already searched half of this patch of islands. Surely it isn't here?" a sailor said. Hans glared at him.

"We have to search *all* of the islands," he said frustratedly. "We must find it or else."

"Whatever."

Then the dream shifted. In this second dream, he was still hovering over Hans and Nolan, but this time they looked worried about something. Then, a tiger shark erupted out of the water near their boat and bit a part of a handrail off at the side of the boat and leaped back into the water. Hans, Nolan and two sailors backed off from the broken handrail, when a great white shark leaped out of the water and almost bit off one of the sailors' hands. Hans took out his pistol, drew his sword, and Nolan took out his shotgun. Just as another tiger shark erupted out of the sea, with one slice of Hans' sword the shark was beheaded. Then, a few more sharks tried to attack, but these were all killed by the demons.

"Whew," one of the sailors stammered. "That was... close." Nolan nodded.

"I think we should end this stupid mission."

"Shut up," Hans grumbled. Then James woke up.

At that time, the others were all sitting by the fire and eating food. The rain had stopped.

"James!" called Marcus. "You finally woke up!"

"What time is it?" James asked.

"We found a stream not far into the forest," Peter said. "I managed to catch some fish." Then he handed James a piece of fish skewered by a stick.

"Thanks," James said. When they had all finished eating, the group packed up their tents and their packs and ventured into the forest.

They had walked for twenty minutes when Alex asked, "Is there any water around here?" Peter thought for a minute.

"Plants store water," he said. "I don't know if it works, but maybe you could cut a plant in half and let the water inside its stem drip into your mouth? The stream is far to the right-hand side of us, and we would waste time going there." Alex tried drinking from the stem of a nearby banana plant.

"It worked," she said. "How did you know that plants have so much water inside them?"

"I just know it," Peter said.

"Okay," James said, "the deeper into the forest we venture, there should be more bases and traps set by the demons."

"Right," Liliana said, "and Gremword should also be able to create some 'natural disasters' in our path, like hurricanes and avalanches, and he could also turn some of these snow-topped mountains-" she pointed to a mountain range, "into volcanoes. With all those threats, I'm scared."

"Hey," James spoke, "there are some footprints there. They look like...tigers?"

"No," Peter hesitated, and exclaimed, "that's human, no, demon footprints! These prints are quite old, maybe two days ago. Then they should have already reached one of their bases, if they keep going straight."

"But why should we care about whether they've reached their base or not?" asked Marcus.

"I'm just telling you that," Peter said. "It might be useful in the future."

After an hour, they had reached a small, short mountain range.

"Could we take a rest?" asked Alex.

"Just a little further," James said. Alex reluctantly didn't say anything. They stopped at the foot of one of the mountains. Slowly the rainforest faded away to a temperate one, and they sat down and rested.

"It's noon," Peter pointed at the sun. "How about we hunt something for lunch?"

"There are some berries," Liliana spotted. At the edge of the rainforest stood a clump of bushes, with clusters of blackberries hanging around. "I'll go pick some of them," she said. "While you two could hunt something."

"And I'll make a fire," Alex said.

"Good. James, come with me," Peter said. "I found some deer tracks. Let's follow it."

"OK." They followed behind the deer for a few minutes, when they heard the burble of a stream. When they looked through the bushes and leaves, they saw a deer happily drinking freshwater from a stream. They slowly approached the deer, with their weapons in their hands, and then quickly struck. James swiftly engulfed the deer with water, and Peter's arrow lodged deep in its skull. Then James cut the animal's flesh into pieces, hefted it over their shoulders, and trudged back through the undergrowth to their camp. Meanwhile, Marcus made a campfire easily.

When they had returned, a blazing fire had already been built in an area cleared of bushes and undergrowth. On the floor were piles of blackberries, and the resting champions. As James and Peter entered the clearing, Marcus was the first to notice them.

"Hey, James! You finally came back!" Alex smirked.

"Don't speak to them like that."

"We found a river!" James announced. "And a deer was drinking beside it, so we killed it."

"Finally, we have some proper food," Marcus said. When the group was eating the cooked deer, James started to think about the other champions' powers.

Finally, he asked, "I've been thinking, what powers do you have? I have water powers and Peter has desert powers, but what about the rest of you?" Alex looked up from her food.

"I can control and bend most winds," she said. "But why do you care?"

"Well...I kind of wanted to know which powers you, Marcus and Liliana had, so that I would know...what you could do..."

"Okay," Marcus made a small flame appear in his hand. "I can control fire, make it spread, disappear, and even control its temperature."

"And I can heal very well," Liliana said. "If I say specific phrases or do specific movements, I can heal bruises, wounds... But what about you?"

"Me? I can control most liquids and breathe in water. But I don't know what else I can do."

After a short meal, everyone felt rested and decided to move on. As they ascended the mountain that stood in front of them like a silent, unmoving giant, the forest slowly faded away to meagre clumps of bushes and rocks. Soon, they were tiredly trudging upward on a steep path, and as James looked down, he could see the shore of Alemis.

"We should make camp on top of the mountains," Marcus suggested, but Peter shook his head.

"If we camp there," he said, "then the demons on the other side of the mountains will easily see us. It may be safer to camp in a cave."

"I see a cave over there," Alex said, pointing to a hole in a cliff.

"Where?" James searched the mountain. "Oh...there. But how do we get there? It's hollowed out of the mountainside." Alex thought about that. Then, when she pushed at the air around her, James felt a gust of wind blow around them, and onto a pile of rocks beside their path. The rocks flew toward the cave and then formed a narrow path just wide enough for them to walk on leading to the cave. Alex repeated the process, and soon she had created a safe bridge for them, all connected to the cliff, but it must've used much of Alex's energy because her face turned pale. When the last of them stumbled into the cave, Peter had started rubbing two thick tree branches together to make fire.

"What are you doing?" asked Marcus.

"Making a fire," Peter replied. "We need it for light, torches, cooking food, and warmth. It is essential for us."

"I have some food," James said. "Pieces of raw deer."

When Marcus looked out of the cave, the sun was setting.

"I'll explore further into this cave," Marcus said. Peter grabbed a stick; made it catch fire in the campfire and tossed it to Marcus.

"Make use of it as a torch," Peter said. Marcus smiled and walked into the depths of the cave. James looked at their surroundings.

"Let's set up our tents," he said. The quest group got out their tents, threw them on the ground and started setting up their campsite, around the blazing fire. A few minutes later, Marcus returned to the tents.

When Peter asked him about how deep the cave was, he said, "There are several tunnels leading out of this chamber. I explored one of these, but it seemed to go on forever, so I came back."

"We'll investigate these tunnels in the morning," James said. "First, we'll finish setting up the campsite… and have some dinner."

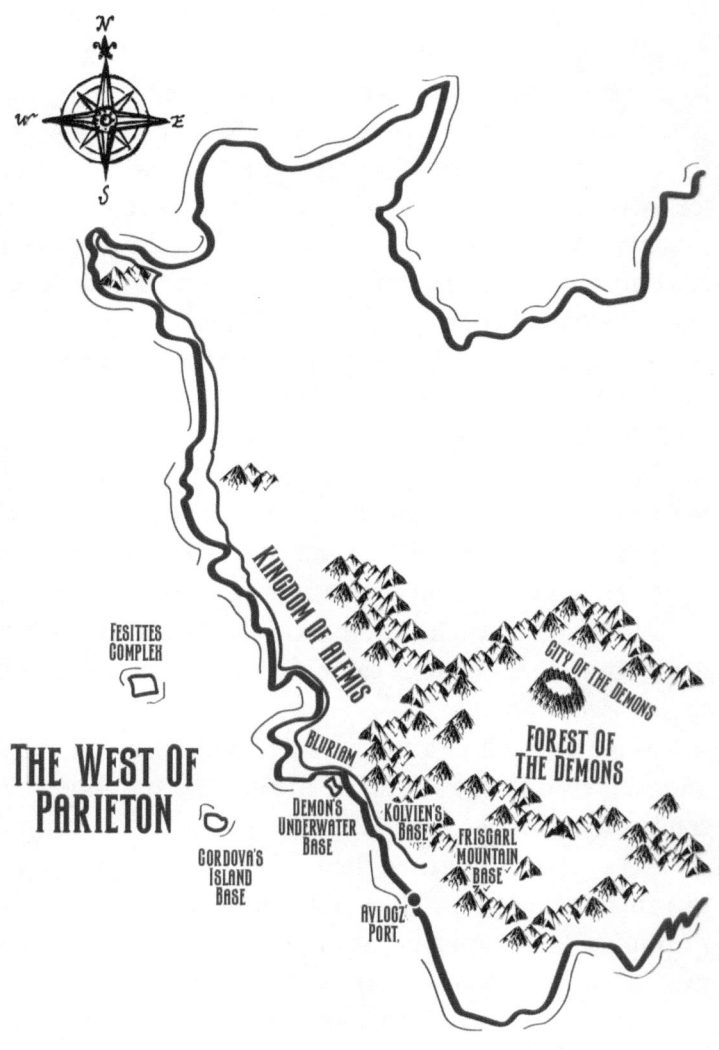

Eleven
Prisoner

After the quest group had eaten all the deer meat, they decided to rest and sleep. Alex took the first watch, followed by Marcus at one in the morning. The rest of them went to sleep, and James strangely did not have dreams.

The next morning, before the sun even rose, the quest group packed up their tents and laid them in a corner. As Liliana argued that they should walk over the mountains, James and Marcus both said, "There might be a way to the other side of the mountains in the tunnels!" Peter and Alex also agreed with them, so Liliana reluctantly followed them further into the cave, holding their torches, looking straight ahead.

"Here," Marcus suddenly pointed to a tunnel leading from the entrance chamber. "I explored this tunnel."

"Let's go in," Alex said.

The group entered the passage, and Liliana muttered in a low voice," I hate tunnels."

"Why?" asked James.

"They're scary," Liliana said. "Scary and dark." A few minutes later, they heard a trickling sound, like water.

"Finally!" shouted Marcus. "I've almost died of thirst." Alex snickered at him but didn't say anything. After they turned the next corner, a huge underground lake appeared out of the darkness in front of them. As they rushed to drink water, James made an enormous mistake, and that was lifting water, then dropping it.

The sound of the water dropping echoed across the chamber, rebounding against every wall. Then, the sound travelled through a tunnel, into a secret demon base. As the leader of the group of demons over there, General Kolvien, heard the sound and cried, "What was that?" The demons in his throne room froze.

"It must be someone in the base, showering or bathing or something," one of his servants said.

"No," Kolvien said. He feared the noise; it sounded like someone was messing in his base's entrance.

"It's just a splash of water," a demon said, and then went back to doing their regular job.

"Investigate the tunnel!" Kolvien ordered.

"Fine," his attendant sighed and pointed to five demons. "You five, come with me." The demons slowly sauntered down the tunnel, sure that there were no intruders there.

Beside the lake, the quest group had heard the demons' shouts.

"Who made the sound?" Liliana asked uncertainly. Nobody moved.

"It looks like they're coming for us," Peter said.

"So, we kill them?" Marcus asked.

"Sure," James said, "let's kill them."

"Did you even think," Peter said, "that they could muster a superior force? And if they don't return to their base, then their leader would suspect something."

"James could flood their base," Marcus said.

"No," Alex said, "we should only attack them if they attack us first." James suddenly realised that Marcus hadn't made a wise choice.

"Alex is right," James agreed.

But then, the demons that General Kolvien sent out arrived at the cave, and one was saying, "See? Nobody here." The rest of them widened their eyes.

Another one said, "No, dummy. There are intruders." Then all the demons noticed the quest group.

"Charge!" the demons yelled. "Kill them!"

"I'll handle that," James said. James summoned an enormous tidal wave out of the lake and threw it towards the demons and then wrapped them up in a water cocoon. The wave washed the demons into the lake, and James used the water's pressure to keep the demons underwater, until they died. "Piece of cake," James said. But then, the group heard a shout from the tunnel that the demons had come from. Then they heard footsteps that became louder and louder until a troop of around seventy demons arrived at the cave. When they saw the group, they raised their weapons and charged.

The whole group used their powers in this fight. Alex summoned winds that knocked demons off their feet, but they always stood up again. Marcus summoned flames that tried but failed to engulf the demons. Peter summoned a sandstorm, which engulfed the demons, but the demons quickly darted out of it and kept on fighting. James summoned tidal waves, but the demons didn't seem to be bothered by that. And troop after troop of demon soldiers arrived at the battle. Finally, Kolvien himself arrived at the scene, when James was darting across a wall, pursued by ten demons, and Alex did a backflip on a sharp stone, and she only just got away from five demons. Kolvien was the most powerful of all. He swung his axe like it was part of his body, and when he drove it to the floor the stone and rocks around him cracked under the force. After a few minutes, the quest group was trapped and circled by demons and were brought to Kolvien's base.

"You will be put in the dungeons!" Kolvien shouted, grinning evilly. "But first, you must tell us why you were trespassing on our demonic territory." Marcus opened his mouth to speak, but Alex stopped him.

"We were just passing by," James hastily said.

"And you ventured into these mountains," Kolvien said. "I wonder where you are going. And I have never heard of any humans who could fight so well." James gulped. He didn't have a response. "Put them in cages!" Kolvien ordered. Several guards came and told them to follow, and three soldiers walked behind them. As they passed through the base, James spotted several storerooms. Barrels were stacked in there, and so were chests, logs, weapons and other things. Deeper into the base, James heard muffled, terrified screams, as if people were in pain. Finally, they arrived at the quest group's cell.

There was nothing in the cell, except for dust and tiny rocks. The guards kicked the door close.

"Enjoy your stay!" They laughed and walked away. Alex stamped her foot in anger.

"Look at the mess we're in now!"

Peter gazed out of a barred window, which was one of their only means of escape, while Liliana said, "We could escape," but it sounded like she was trying to convince herself. James looked out of the window as well. They were on a steep mountainside, and if they somehow broke the bars on the windows they would just fall and die. That way wasn't going to work. But maybe if they went the other way, then maybe there would be a slight chance of escape… And then James had an idea!

"We could escape," he said. The others stared at him, shocked.

"What???"

"When they bring us food," James explained, "we could knock them out and look for somewhere to escape. They won't be expecting an attack."

"But how are you sure that they'll bring us food?" Peter asked.

"I mean, like, *if* they bring us food," James said. Then they heard two demons opening the door to their cell, holding a tray of bread and water. They threw the tray onto the floor.

Before the demon could leave, James grabbed his ankle and pulled backwards, making him fall. His companions, who were standing outside, stepped back in shock. After one second, they drew swords and advanced toward the quest group. But then, Alex commanded a strong wind to both blow toward the demons and the other quest members, which propelled them to the corridor outside. Unfortunately, the other demons heard the banging, and all rushed to the scene. Soon, they were cornered and were struggling to dodge the demons' blows.

Then Kolvien walked up to the group, and said, "Lock them up again. And take away the food that you just brought them. They won't need it." Then he focused on James. "Don't forget to guard them day and night." Then he strode away, leaving the demons to throw the group back in the cell.

Every one of them were angry at James in the cell.

"Your foolish plan took away all the water!" Marcus roared.

"And," Peter added, "they're now guarding us! We can't escape anymore." James slowly walked to the other side of the prison room, and lay down to sleep, despite his thirstiness. Then he dreamed about Hans and Nolan... again. They were on their boat, heading toward yet another island.

"Steer toward the island in the southwest," Hans ordered. A sailor turned the steering wheel, and the boat lurched forward and picked up speed.

Hans pulled out a phone from his pocket and lifted it to his ear. "-ave less than three weeks to find it," a voice inside the phone said. "And bye!" A sailor looked at him.

"Less than three weeks?" He shook his head. "We must hurry!" Nolan looked up and yawned.

"Less than three weeks," he said. "How exciting. The end to this stupid, meaningless mission is close, and we will finally stop wasting our time."

"Why did I even bring this man?" Hans muttered. Then James woke.

When he woke up, sunlight was streaming into their cell, and Peter was sitting in the corner, but everyone else was sleeping. Peter looked up.

"Sorry for being mad at you," he said. James didn't say anything. He knew that it was his fault. Peter looked out of the window and said, "I have another plan."

"What?" James leaned closer to Peter. "Tell me."

Peter raised up a wooden stick and said, "We use this stick to get the keys out of the guard's pocket. Then we reach out of the bars, unlock the gate, and sneak out!"

"Great plan," James said. "I'll wake the others." They both nodded and prodded the others awake. Very soon, they were all watching James as he poked the guards' pockets and took out two small, dusty keys. But unfortunately, the guards woke up because of the movement and rushed to check the cell. Without thinking, Peter snatched the keys from James and tossed them out of the window. Marcus scrambled over and threw the stick to a corner of the room just as the guards opened the door.

"What are you guys doing?" one guard questioned.

The other guard said, "You were poking us. We felt it; we weren't asleep at all. And you took our keys. Where are they?"

"I threw them out of the window," Peter hastily said.

"Did you?" The guards queried. "David, bring him to the torture room." The other guard shoved Peter, who was screaming, out of their cell, and walked with him to the torture room.

Just as David was leaving, James lunged at him, bringing him to the ground. As Marcus uppercut the other guard, Alex came with a flying front kick to David's jaw, knocking him unconscious. Liliana then punched the nerve point between the remaining guard's ribs, and as he howled Liliana swiftly shut his mouth. They laid the guards, unconscious, on the ground, and after freeing Peter they set out through the base. The demon base was an endless maze of corridors. Twice they ducked into dark rooms to avoid demons. Finally, as they left the dungeon, they saw a barred window.

"That must be it," Peter said. Then they heard footsteps behind them, saw three demons and tried to run away. But as the demons closed the gate, James realised that they were trapped in a cell, with no way out except for the window. And they had entered it by themselves.

"Welcome to your new cell," the demons said and handed them a tray of biscuits and a jug of water.

"Water!" Alex gasped and quickly drank the water. After one gulp, however, she spat it out. "It's saltwater!"

"Yes," the demons smirked. "Enjoy it!" And they left the cell. Liliana sat down.

"We can't lose hope."

Marcus sighed, "We might spend the rest of our lives in these dungeons." James looked around the room, but it was empty. Outside the window, the sun had risen to its zenith and would soon be setting. He glanced at Alex. She was sitting in the corner of the room, staring at the floor and muttering to herself. James looked at where she was looking and saw a crack in the floor. Alex reached out her head and squinted into the crack, shook her head and sat down again. James turned to Peter.

"There's a crack in the floor." Peter walked over to James.

"What? Where? Oh, there. Hmm. Maybe we should try that?" Marcus heard them.

"The crack? I can summon up fire to see in there." He slowly went over and shot flames into the darkness of the hole. They all crowded around to see...nothing. Even with the flames, it was just an endless darkness.

"We need a stone," Peter said. Then, he explained, "We drop the stone into the hole, and see if the sound is distant or not." James looked around for a stone. Instead, Alex used her wind powers to blow a smooth, tiny pebble into the hole.

For a moment, nothing happened, but then the group heard a sharp, "Ow!"

For a few seconds, they were stunned. Then the voice repeated, "Ow!" James then heard a thunk, footsteps and a face appeared in the hole. It was that of an old man, with white eyebrows and a bald head. But his eyes told the group that he wasn't a demon.

"Who are you?" Liliana asked.

The old man looked above him for a second and asked, "You know that already. You are a demon."

"We're not," James said. "We've been thrown into this cell by demons."

The man studied the group and said, "I am a human. I have been in this prison for seven years."

"What is your name?" Marcus asked.

The man paused before replying, "I am Theodore. I was wandering through the mountains before accidentally walking near this demon base, when one of their men saw me and put me into this room. Who are you? You're human, right?" The quest group all decided to lie.

"Of course we're human," they said, although only *part* of them was human. The rest was from one of the tribes in the alliance. But then when they introduced themselves, they told the man their actual names.

"We're trying to escape," Alex said. "Is there any way to escape down there in your cell?"

"No," Theodore said.

"So, this will be our grave," Marcus said glumly.

"We can escape," Liliana urged. The sun was already setting; dusk was rolling in. Theodore had retreated to the darkness of his own cell and had fallen asleep. Now, the quest group was in the cell, discussing escape plans. Suddenly, the door flew open, and a piece of bread was thrown in. But James saw ten demons, and they couldn't possibly overcome all of them. But when the demons closed the door, Liliana kicked a stone at the door, so that when it closed there was still a gap.

When the demons left, James said, "Good thinking."

"Yeah," Marcus said. "Let's leave now."

"No," Alex and Peter said in unison. "We must wait till night. That's when they'll least be expecting us." Marcus glared but didn't say anything.

That night they didn't sleep, even though Theodore was snoring. After a few hours, James gestured for them to follow him, and they snuck out of the cell, through winding corridors and, finally, found an exit. They all rushed out, but as Marcus shouted, "Finally," a few demons heard them. They sprinted, pursued, into the other side of the mountain.

Twelve
Peter's Sandstorm

After a few minutes they were sure that they had lost the demons. They wandered around the area, searching for shelter and food. Finally, they came to an overgrown path lined with blueberry bushes, with a clearing surrounded with undergrowth beside it.

"This is funny," Peter said. "It's almost like someone's been here before."

"We can camp here. It offers food." Marcus said.

"No," James said, even though he was exhausted. "We'd better go further; what if it's a trap?" As they trudged below the bright moon, the forest was as quiet as a stone. After walking for a few minutes, however, James felt like his spine was about to crumble, as did the others, so they were forced to camp where they were for the night. As they set up their tents, the sounds of the forest were annoyingly loud, but these sounds were unlike that of animals. Even though it was obviously different from the normal sounds, they were all too tired to notice. They fell asleep as soon as their heads hit their pillows, and were too tired even to dream, so James had a dreamless night.

James woke early that morning, before the sun had even begun to rise, and he immediately noticed that their packs had disappeared. It was a cave full of stalactites, with nothing in it except for them. Beside James, Peter, Alex, Marcus and Liliana were sleeping…but where were their packs? James stood up and looked around the area, searching for their things, but the packs were nowhere to be found. Then, he looked further away, but didn't notice any trace of their packs, until he became aware of a few prints in the dirt, leading to a tree. James walked towards the tree, and saw that their packs were beside it, but they were empty! James scanned around for signs of anything that could have taken the things inside and saw a cluster of buildings - maybe a village - beside a river. They could get some food from the villagers! He brought back the packs and resolved to wake his friends up. Once they were awake, he told them that their packs were empty.

"That's odd," Peter murmured.

"And nothing could have taken them," Alex said.

"Look! There are some bite-marks at the edge of them!" Marcus observed.

"We don't have any food left," Alex said unhappily.

"We might be able to borrow food from the village over there," James pointed in the direction of the village. "And judging by the bites on the bags and the footprints in the ground, I presume that it was an animal."

"Yeah," Marcus agreed. "Let's head towards the village! Like James said, they might offer us food, and we might even stay there for a night or two!"

They headed towards the village. When they were almost there, one of the villagers noticed them and called, "Hey! Who are you?"

"We're travellers," Peter replied. "We got lost in the forest, and we saw your village, so we came because we needed provisions."

"Hmm," the villager muttered and said, "I will take you to the village head," and began walking.

On the way to the village head, Alex whispered to Peter, "Is this really…a good idea?"

"Sure is," Peter said, "and even if they disagree, we can still escape. They're not demons, and they might offer provisions."

"You said *might*." But then it was too late; they had arrived at the village head's house.

The house had two floors and was a bit grander than the others. It was decorated with flowerpots and paintings on paper. The furniture was simple; with a wooden table with two chairs, three lamps, an uncomfortable-looking white bed, a small stove and two plain, wooden cupboards. As they entered the room, the door creaked as it opened.

"Hello," Peter said formally, even before the villager could say anything.

"What do you want?" The village head said. "Why have you five come to this village?"

"Sir," the villager spoke, "they are travellers, or so they said. They got lost in the forest."

"Return to your job, Jonathan. I will sort out this problem." Problem? James thought, as Jonathan left the room. "Sit down," the village head said.

"Sir," Peter said, "we have run out of provisions and-"

"Silence!" The village head growled and took off his mask, revealing the demon Kolvien. "Not only have you escaped my dungeons, but you have killed two of my men! How dare you ask for provisions? Guards-bring them back to their cell!"

"What?" James stammered. "But…" Demons swarmed into the room, in the direction of the group, which bolted for the windows. They climbed out, with a few arrows stuck in their bodies, and without thinking, darted to a river. In the process, one of them caught Marcus on the leg and pulled, but they still managed to swim to the far end of the river and ran.

James didn't know where he was going. All he knew was that he needed to put as much distance as possible between them and the demons. Now that they had recovered from their shock, Alex panted, "Where's Marcus?" Peter couldn't see the demons anymore.

"Did we lose the demons?"

"I saw Marcus being taken by them," James said grimly. Then, the undergrowth behind them exploded with demons.

"Run!" Liliana screamed. Everyone ran, except for Peter, who didn't move.

"Come on!" James called. Suddenly, Peter's eyes started glowing, and sand started raining from the sky. Peter fell to his knees, but James and Alex hefted him up to their shoulders and ran behind Liliana.

"Sandstorm!" a demon coughed.

"Don't lose them!" another one screamed. But they *were* losing them. The demons were already several hundred metres behind. The group had escaped from the group of demons.

Although the group had escaped from Kolvien, they had lost their provisions and their weapons. Alex was also a bit reluctant to continue.

"There must be more bases like that one," she said, "and we might not be able to escape one of them. And Marcus was taken." Peter and James looked at her.

"If we don't kill Gremword, *our* base will be destroyed. We cannot give up now." Liliana looked forward, and saw the endless forest, with dense undergrowth, numerous thorn bushes and towering, thick trees covered with vines. The filthy, muddy ground was dotted with footprints and sticks.

"Come on," Peter urged. As they walked, James winced in pain and held his leg. He looked at his leg, and there was a bleeding cut just centimetres above his knee. Peter saw the cut and motioned for the others to stop.

"Ow," James said.

"I can fix that." Liliana came over and knelt down beside James. She moved her hands in a circular motion, spoke some incantations and the wound partly healed. The bleeding stopped, and a thin, invisible layer of some material had grown over the cut. James stared.

"How did you do that?"

"I have healing powers, James," Liliana said.

"Let's move on," Peter said. "It's the afternoon already." So, the group set off once more, with James feeling much better with his wound healed.

After another few hours of silent trekking through the rough biome, the group stumbled upon some human footprints.

"Someone was here three hours ago," Peter said.

"And which direction did they go?" Alex asked. Peter pointed to their left.

"That direction."

"Let's just ignore the prints and continue on our path," James said. "The opposing mountains are closer to us now."

"These footprints look like...human feet," Peter gasped. "That means that there's a village nearby."

"Or maybe it's just a lost traveller."

"There's another set of footprints!" Liliana said surprisedly. "That means that there are two humans. We could follow the prints."

"But after what happened today, the demons..." Alex said slowly. But James also agreed that they could try it, so Alex had to follow.

"But," she said, "only one of us goes into the village first, if it leads to a village, and see if it's demon-infested or not."

"Right." Then the group set off tracking the humans, or the demons.

After a few minutes they arrived at a river.

"The tracks lead into the river," James said. "Then they disappear."

"He must've drowned," Alex said.

"Or maybe he's a water demon," Peter said. James saw some underwater tracks.

"The tracks continue underwater," he said.

"How did you do that?" the others asked loudly.

"I have water powers," James replied. "The tracks lead in that-" he pointed upstream "-direction."

"Where do they come onto land?" Peter questioned.

"Twenty metres?" James answered uncertainly.

"Great," Alex said. "So, we cross the river and follow the tracks?"

"Yes," Peter said. "There's a log over there. We can use it as a bridge." After three minutes, they had safely reached the other side of the river and found the tracks. Then they tracked it for another twenty minutes and came to a village on a plain.

The village was a widely spread combination of barn houses and huts made of straw and wooden planks. There were several paths leading from one house to the other. But the unsettling thing about the village was that it was dark, and mist seemed to hang in the air.

"Right," James said, "I'll investigate it first." The others waited as he walked into the river and entered a house. He stayed in the hut for a few minutes, and someone escorted him out.

"...no one is outside because there is fog," the villager said. "It is also dinnertime."

"Where are your crops?" James asked. The others looked around and indeed saw no crops or farmland.

"It's autumn," the villager said, "we have harvested them all, and are waiting for the new ones to grow." James didn't think it was autumn; it was more like summer. But maybe it was because of the terrain or the altitude.

"Something's not right," Peter said. "It is not autumn." James also frowned.

"Sorry," he said, "but I have to go."

"That's fine!" the villager said. "Goodbye!" He waved, and James joined the group. He pulled out some pieces of bread from his pocket.

"This is all I managed to get," he said. "There was something not right about the village."

"We sensed it too," Peter agreed. Suddenly, a loud shout came from behind them. They turned to see fifty villagers storming towards them, with weapons in their hands.

The villager that James had talked to yelled, "Charge!"

The group stood there, stunned, for a moment, but James shook them out of their daze. Peter stared at the villagers, and when James looked at them, he realised that they weren't villagers, instead they were demons.

"How could they have regrouped so quickly?" Alex asked, also noticing the demons.

"Probably Kolvien alerted the others," Peter shouted. "But now we should run!" The group sprinted toward the cover of the forest before the demons could capture any of them. They crashed through the undergrowth, pursued by the demons. Liliana spotted a tiny place surrounded by tall bushes and thick undergrowth beside a waterfall, and tackled the others, causing them all to fall into the bushes. The demons ran by, not noticing them.

"That was clo-"

"Shh!!" Peter covered James's mouth. Alex suddenly waved her hand in front of their noses, and they both turned to see her pointing to a small lever covered by layers of mud, which caused Peter to gasp and motion for the rest not to pull it. But Liliana didn't see Peter doing that, grabbed it and pulled.

The ground literally slid from beneath them. The group fell, screaming, into a deep pit. Uh-oh, James thought. This might be our death. But instead, they plummeted straight down the hole and landed on a cold cobblestone floor.

"Ow," someone groaned to James's right.

"What...Where..." someone else moaned beside him.

Then he heard the rustle of clothes and Peter's voice saying, "Where...are...we...?" Above them, faint sunlight spread onto the stone floor, the last light of the sun. Soon it would be dark. Then James struggled up and had the first proper look at the tunnel they were in, which almost freaked him out. A skeleton in chains hung a few metres diagonally above them. Axes and spears dripping blood were stuck in cracks on the wall, and three chests lay five metres beside them. Beside him, Peter was struggling to stand. His limbs were cut and bleeding. Alex and Liliana were lying right next to them, and they had also suffered from numerous wounds. Liliana had a gash on her forehead.

"Well," Peter stammered, "look at this mess."

James and Peter sat down on the floor. After three minutes Alex woke and stared, half-conscious, at her surroundings, and then at her wounds.

"Where is this place?"

Peter smiled.

"No idea." Then Alex glanced at Liliana.

"Is...she alive?" James put his finger in front of Liliana's nose and felt her breathing.

"She's breathing," James said. But she seems to be stunned or something.

"Good," Peter said, "she'll become conscious later."

Thirteen
The Tunnel

After a few minutes, the three children were sitting beside a blazing fire, nursing their wounds, but Liliana still hadn't regained consciousness.

"You know," James said, "I do think this quest is becoming a bit...hopeless. Maybe we shouldn't have come here after all."

"Don't think like that!" Peter urged. "If we don't kill Gremword, everyone in our base will eventually be defeated and killed, along with all the other normal men and the tribes. Do you want that to happen?"

"Of course not," Alex and James said in unison.

"You could go to sleep," Peter said. "As I said, I'll take the first watch."

"Right," Alex sighed, and then yawned. She curled up on the floor and immediately started snoring.

"You should sleep too, James."

"You know," James said, "this place is beginning to freak me out. I mean...it's like a massacre has happened here hundreds of years ago. And...there may still be something here." Peter nodded wearily.

"But you should sleep now. We'll have a long day ahead of us tomorrow." James nodded and fell asleep on the cold floor.

That night, James had a dream about Hans and Nolan again. They were on their boat, heading to an island that seemed to be one of the last in the chain of islands.

"Almost there," Hans said, "and it's the second to last island. If we don't find them in this island chain, then we'll head southwest and double-check over there. We'll sail it all over again."

"NOOOOOO!" Nolan shouted. "WHYYYY?"

"Because we have to double check, dummy," Hans grumbled. "Lord Gremword said so. And shuddup." One of the sailors turned to Hans.

"I saw a glint of gold!"

"Gold?" Hans asked.

"It reflected the sunlight! It must be on the island that we're heading to!" As Hans shook his head and tried to see the gold, the dream darkened and changed into something else.

It was a battle in a tunnel. Two great armies fought, and James recognised one army as the demons. The other army was, well...they weren't demons, and they weren't human. The armies clashed, spears dripping blood, but slowly the battle turned to the demons' favour. They were winning. James watched as the demons slowly destroyed the other army, until there was only one person, obviously the army leader...left. The demons were about to kill him when their demon lord yelled, "Don't kill him!" The demons looked over.

"Why?"

"Because," their lord explained, "we want him to *suffer*. What would you say if I made him immortal, so that he could suffer eternal punishment and agony for daring to lead this pathetic army here and trying to wipe us out?" The demons cheered and agreed with their lord, while the other army's leader's eyes widened in horror. They dragged their captive away, laughing and pointing at him. When James woke, it was morning.

When he woke, the sun was already pretty high in the sky, but not at its zenith. Peter and Alex were talking about their plans for the day, and Liliana, who seemed to be thinking, was sitting in the corner.

When Peter saw James awake, he called, "Hey James! You woke!"

Alex looked over and said, "You don't have to act so surprised." Liliana stood up and walked to James.

"It's about time you woke up."

"Liliana came around in the middle of the night," Peter said. "We're now thinking about moving forward in the tunnel, because I don't think we could go back to ground level. It's a deep hole." James suddenly noticed something. The blood, the weapons…the tunnel that they were in looked like the tunnel of the battle!

"Peter," he said, "last night I had a dream, and it was about a battle in a tunnel. One side was the demons, and one side was another army. Anyway, the demons won, but they took one captive and sentenced him to eternal punishment and agony. And…the tunnel the battle was in looked like this tunnel."

"This tunnel?" Peter asked. "Then, maybe the captive or whatever he was is still here." James hadn't thought of this. Maybe, if the captive was down here, and he fought the demons, then the group might be able to seek help from him.

When James told Peter and Alex that the captive of the demons could help the group, they disagreed.

"The demons could also be down here as well. That just makes this tunnel more dangerous."

"But we could rescue him," James said. "Anyway, I think we should explore this tunnel now."

"Good idea," Liliana said. "We aren't going to get anywhere if we just stay here."

"Yeah," Alex changed her mind. "Let's move on."

"But we don't have provisions," Peter complained. "There is no food, no-"

"Do you think we're going to find food by waiting?" In the end, Peter followed them into the darkness.

As they walked further into the tunnel, it became darker and spookier. Every gust of wind sounded like an opposing demon, and each twig snapping beneath their feet like a monster. The small area lit by their dim torches was covered with blood and bones.

"How much further?" Liliana asked, shivering with both coldness and fear.

"I don't know," James said. "I don't know when we'll find an exit." Then, out of the gloom, an arched doorway appeared in the wall. James looked into the doorway, but he didn't see anything.

"W-where does that lead to?" Peter asked fearfully.

"I don't know," James replied. "But I doubt…that it would be something good." A cry came from inside the doorway, which made the four back off.

"I think we should a-avoid that doorway," Liliana stammered. "Let's continue down this tunnel." Blood dripped from the ceiling as the rest agreed with Liliana to avoid the doorway, but the cry came from the doorway once more. James listened more closely and felt that the cry was not an angry one, but it was more like whatever was in there was crying for help. Don't be fooled by a cry, James told himself. The demons have tricked you enough times for you to know that. And his friends were leaving the doorway. Maybe he *should* leave the tunnel alone. But curiosity took over. Without even calling for his friends, he stepped forwards into the gloom.

James walked deep into the tunnel, searching for the place that the cry came from. He had walked around for minutes when he arrived at another corridor, crisscrossing with the one he was in. He stepped into the other corridor and saw a horrible thing; an old man with a long beard was being roasted alive, on a bronze platform on top of a fire. The platform was covered by a layer of thorns, real thorns that pierced the man's body. And in his mouth, there was an enormous ball that stretched his jaws, but he was forced to keep it all in his mouth. As the man screamed in pain and agony, James saw the man's body glowing faintly. He sprinted forward to help the man, but suddenly an invisible force collided with him and caused James to stagger back. Suddenly a snakelike voice spoke.

"Ahh, a visitor."

James spun around. "What?" he thought. That couldn't have been the man. But then the voice spoke again.

"Another victim for my brilliant torture device." These words both surprised and scared James greatly. Was he going to be tortured? But first, he wanted to figure out who it was. He looked down the corridor and saw nothing unusual. Then, when he looked again, a glow began to filter through one of the walls. As he nervously backed away from the man and the light, the wall behind him started to rumble. He fearfully edged away from the walls and down the corridor. But then, part of the floor gave way, opening a fissure one metre in front of him. An arrow shot from the far end of the corridor, opposite the fissure, but James dodged it. Holding his breath, he retreated to the tortured man. If there was a fight, he thought, then he'd be dead. He didn't even have weapons, and if demons attacked him, he'd be dangerously outnumbered. Then the walls beside him crumbled, and a few dozen armed demons stepped out of the gloom, surrounding James.

Alex, Liliana and Peter hadn't noticed that James wasn't with them as they thought he was following them. They'd walked very far when they realised James was not with them.

"Wait," Peter suddenly said, "where's James?" The others looked around them, but there was no sign of James anywhere.

"Where is he?" Alex asked.

"Maybe," Liliana thought aloud, "James went into the doorway that we found."

"If he went in there," Peter said, "well, I guess we should backtrack and find him." Suddenly a fissure opened on the ground beside them, and three arrows sped out of the darkness. The stone walls began to glow, and after a minute they crumbled, revealing around eighty demons swarming towards them.

"I guess we're in trouble," Alex said.

"Certainly," Peter said.

As the demons rushed towards James, with their weapons' blades glistening, all he thought was to defend himself. Before the demons could reach him, he leaped into the air, kicked a wall and landed behind the demons. Confused, the demons turned, but James rocketed into the air before they could react. One demon threw his spear, and James grabbed hold of it. Right, James thought. As he soared above the mass of demons, an arrow flew through the air. James tried to deflect it, but he was out of practice. It pierced his elbow, and the demons roared in delight. But their delight turned into anger when James hurled the spear and killed a demon. Seven demons shot arrows, but all of them missed. James tried to fly further, but he landed right in front of the fissure. The demons surged forward and attempted to impale him, but he slid through the crowd of demons and stopped in the middle. Since he was underneath them, the demons walked around, trying to find him, but then he tripped five of them with his leg, and kicked into the air. He grabbed hold of a sword in the process and stuck it into a crack in the wall. But then the leader of the demons approached them and threw a net towards James. He tried to dodge it, but the net trapped James. He dropped like a sack of potatoes to the ground. The tortured man made a noise that sounded like, "Help," but the demons' leader grunted, "Shut up."

The demons in front of Peter, Alex and Liliana shot their arrows, hefted their spears and readied their swords. As their line of shields rushed toward them, Alex summoned wind to attack the demons, but they just kept charging. Then she backflipped and landed behind them, causing confusion to spread over the demons. Then part of them rushed towards Alex, and the other demons towards the others. Peter's eyes glowed once, and sand sprouted from the tunnel's ceiling, raining down on top of the fight. While the demons were trying to figure out where the group was, Peter grabbed Alex and Liliana and sprinted down the tunnel, leaving the demons and the noise of the fights behind. However, Peter, Alex and Liliana encountered another three dozen demons in the tunnel after a few minutes. And this group was made of a type of stronger, bigger, more powerful demons, each armed with a large axe and a heavy shield. They charged, and after a few seconds the first group of demons joined the other demons and surrounded the group. Even though Alex blasted one of them off his feet, after another few minutes, the demons defeated the three and carried them in sacks to the demons' base.

James was also about to be captured and defeated by the demons. They were more powerful and there were more demons. Despite all his kicks, stabs and throws, the demons still wounded him twice. While he darted around in the tunnel, he tripped, fell and one demon caught him in a net.

"Good move, Darren!" someone in the crowd of demons shouted.

Darren grinned evilly. "I suppose our lord shall appreciate this!" James felt a shiver run down his spine. Their lord? "Now, carry him there quickly." A demon with a crown stepped forward, in front of all the other demons and Darren.

"Gremword shall indeed be pleased for his capture but also be quick about it. Take him there!"

Two demons carried James away in his net, while the demon with the crown grumbled, "What shall we do with it?"

Peter, Alex and Liliana were carried through a secret passageway out of the tunnel, and into fresh sunlight. At first it was blinding, but after only a few seconds they submerged into the ground again. After a few minutes, a door finally appeared in the tunnel, and the demon wearing the crown touched the door, and it opened, revealing a massive underground courtyard. Except that this courtyard had no plants or trees; it was full of demon soldiers drilling, practising, or duelling each other. Behind the courtyard was a wide river and three small drawbridges leading to a gate in the distance. As they approached the gate, the soldiers stared at them as if they were from outer space. Then, they went across the river, inside the gate and continued inside a small passage. They arrived at a crossroads five minutes later and turned left. As they went further into the base, James realised that they were going uphill. Then, suddenly, one demon held out a hand and they all stopped. Arrows erupted from holes in the wall, lodging in front of them. Then they continued. Finally, they reached a sign that said, throne room. They turned right and entered the room.

The same thing happened to James. He was also carried into the base, across the river, into the gate, turned left, turned right and was thrown into the throne room. He heard the loud creak of the stone door behind him as the demons closed it. Only one person came in after him, and he was the demon with the crown. Then James had his first view of the throne room. Three huge chandeliers and thirty torches lit up the room, and two enormous thrones stood at the far end. The walls were lined with statues, paintings and soldiers, and there was a shelf behind the thrones. Upon it lay documents, books and papers, and two armour stands were beside it. Weapons lay in racks on the ceiling, bound in ropes. Two doors were in the corners, one was marked *punishments,* and one was marked *entertainment.* But perhaps the most confident and dominating thing in the room was the demon on the throne. He had a crown of solid gold, fierce brown eyes and muscular limbs. A large, heavy sword was in his scabbard, which was made of lionskin. As he spoke, his voice filled the room.

"Who is this person you have here?"

The demon that came in with James replied, "He has been found in the tunnel, my lord. Quite close to this mountain, and your palace."

"How did he get to the tunnel in the first place?"

"I don't know, my lord. All I know is that he has been wandering in the tunnel."

"Alone?"

"With them." The demon beside James pointed toward the side of the throne room, where three sacks were thrown on the floor.

"You can leave now." The demon beside James bowed to his lord and left the room. "Now," the lord boomed, "tell me why you are here."

James told the tall lord that he was just a normal boy, lost in the vast forest. But the lord didn't believe him.

"I have never seen any mortal man fight like that," he thundered. "I suppose that you are *not* a mortal man after all?" James staggered backwards a step.

"I, er, am trained in martial arts, and-um…" The demon lord stood up and took a step towards James.

"You are NOT a mortal man! However trained you are, it is impossible for a mortal man to have such incredible fighting skills, or to come this close to the emperor Gremword. Now, tell me the truth, or you will be forced to endure eternal torture!" James thought nervously about what type of torture that he would endure.

"I was only lost," James said, "and I fought the demons to defend myself. I am…not mortal-"

"You are not mortal!" the lord boomed. "Then, what are you?"

"I-don't-know-"

"You don't know!" Then, he turned to his demon general and commanded, "Take him to the prison and see if he can remember anything overnight. And if he doesn't, then he will endure eternal torture too!" As James walked out the room, the last thing he saw was the demon lord pointing to the three sacks on the floor, ordering his soldiers to untie them and bring them in front of him. Then, the demons slammed the door shut.

Fourteen
Captured and Escaped (again)

Alex, Peter and Liliana were brought in front of the demon lord.

"Why were you three walking through the tunnel?" he boomed.

Peter said nervously, "We were just lost."

"Lost," the demon repeated. "The other boy also said that he was lost. I think you three are not mortal kids?"

"We are," Liliana said. "We lived in a village, but yesterday we took a walk around, and we got lost."

"So how did you happen to be in the tunnel?" the lord thundered. "The nearest village is also kilometres away."

"Um-" Alex stammered.

The demon lord shouted, "Take them away! Lock them up in different cells so that they can't communicate! And if they don't remember what they were doing here, then they shall be tortured!"

That night, James thought desperately about a plan for escaping. It was already hours after he had been thrown into the small prison cell that he was inside, and he still hadn't thought of anything. He decided to look out of the barred window once more. When he'd been thrown in, he realised the base was on a mountain, overlooking the vast forest below. His cell was on a cliff on the summit of the mountain, so even if he broke through the bars he would still have to climb down the cliff. Then, he looked through the other window. In the cell there were two windows, one overlooking the forest, and one looking over the other side of the mountains,

134

where there was…another forest. But this forest was filled with lights scattered around, and houses, and palaces. It was like a little city, surrounded by mountains which acted as walls. And he realised that the city was full of demons, little dots moving around the landscape. He could also see other small windows and doors in the mountains. As James stood there, looking at the vast forest full of demons, he felt helpless against the armies of them.

But then, in the distance, he saw a strange thing. It looked like a spurt of flame, shooting up into the sky. Then a roar went up below, all the demons shouted. James looked again, and he thought he saw a snakelike tail flick through the trees. Then the demons returned to doing their things. James sat on the floor again, thinking desperately about a plan for escaping. But Gremword was in the centre of the forest, which meant he was in the city. James shook his head, thinking about how he would reach Gremword, if he escaped the prison, how he would reach the middle of the demons' city.

Then he looked outside again, and saw a barred window, facing upwards diagonally, right below him! Because he wanted to know who was in there, he dropped a tiny pebble through the bars, and into the cell below. Two seconds later, a face showed in the bars, that of an old man. The old man had a long beard, and he squinted as he looked at James.

"What were you thinking?" he asked, but his tone surprised James. It was impossible for such a frail man to have had such a powerful voice! James was so surprised that he backed away from the window. "What were you thinking?" he repeated. "Dropping a stone through my window, almost hitting my head!"

"I…didn't mean to do that, …sir." The old man laughed, with an angry glint to his eye.

"Sir?" he asked. "I am not a *sir* anymore, even though I was one before. I am just an old man, locked in prison."

"But why were you locked in the prison?" James asked. The old man ceased laughing.

"What about you?"

James stared at the man, and found himself saying, "I came to kill the demon Gremword, to prevent him from killing my friends, and destroying our base…"

"I also came to kill Gremword, centuries ago," the old man said. "But my force was defeated, all my soldiers killed. I alone was spared, to be tortured eternally."

"How did you live so long?" James asked. It was only later that he realised that it was a bit rude.

The old man said, "The demons made me immortal, with a sort of potion, and tortured me. It was a combination of three of the most painful torture methods ever invented, and I have been tortured for around one thousand years."

James gasped but then asked, "Then, why were you put in this prison?"

136

"I don't know. But I don't like to talk about my torture. It's a painful subject." James sat down on the floor of his cell and resumed thinking about plans for escaping.

Later that night, around three o'clock, the demons had all gone to sleep. All the fires were dimmed, and James' eyes were bloodshot from tiredness. A few ants crawled around his bars, searching for food, but there was no movement elsewhere. James lay down on the cold, wet stone floor and tried to relax. He could escape; he told himself. Think. Then he focused his eyes on the ants, watching them move around. One of them was crawling into cracks in the floor and coming out again. Then the same ant crawled onto the walls just for fun, and as his eyes followed the ant's path, he noticed it crawling into a tiny hole in the wall. Although it was tiny, it was also deep and might've reached the cell beside James's cell. He looked through the hole and saw nothing, so he called, "Hello?"

The other two champions and Peter were both thinking about escape plans, but they'd come up with nothing. Peter was getting impatient, and he banged his fist on the ground. Liliana decided to sleep for energy the following day. Alex was also thinking of escape plans, but she didn't know that she was accidentally placed in the cell right next to James's cell, and it was a surprise for her when she heard James saying, "Hello?" She searched for the source of the sound around the room, while James thought that there was nothing on the other side of the hole after all.

Then Alex said, "Where was that?" Then James listened through the hole.

"Who are you?"

"Who are you?"

"You say who you are first."

"Why should I do that? You say it first." James sighed.

"Fine. My name is James."

"And I'm Alex."

"It's you?"

"What do you mean?"

"There is someone called Alex who is on a quest with me to kill Gremword."

"Yes, it's me. And have you thought of any escape plans?"

"No. What about you?"

"No," Alex said. "But it's good that we can both talk to each other now."

"Yeah. The main problem is how to break out of this stupid prison cell. Then escaping is easy."

"Easy?" Alex shouted, a bit angry. "There's that long way down, and after we escape, we also have to kill Gremword. We also have to get past that stupid city, full of demons!"

James and Alex had exchanged ideas for an hour at least, but they still hadn't thought of anything, and they were getting extremely frustrated. But then, James had an excellent idea.

"Since the doors of our cells are both made of wood," James said, "we could burn them down!"

"Right," Alex said, "but what do we do after we escape from our cells? We still have to get to Peter and Liliana. Then comes the climb down into the demons' city."

"I say that we don't do it just yet," James said. As he was saying that he grabbed a stick from the floor and rubbed it against another stick. Once the sticks caught fire, he passed one stick to Alex and told her to hold it just for a while. Then he looked at the steep mountain and the forest below, deciding which route they should take and where they should both go, and passed the information to Alex. Then, they both set fire to their doors, but when the doors were burning, other parts of their cells caught fire and burned.

Both James and Alex jumped backwards in panic.

"What are we going to do?" James said, a little too loudly. Alex froze, because she heard some voices a few stories below.

"Now they heard us," she whispered fiercely. James considered the problem, but then he suddenly thought about his water powers - he concentrated with all his strength to bring water up to his cell, and seconds later a wave came roaring. The water doused everything in both his and Alex's cell.

"That was close," James said.

Now that the doors were burned down, they stepped out and started searching for Peter and Liliana. It was not an easy search. Luckily, each cell's door had a tiny keyhole, through which Alex or James could see, but most of the cells were either empty or too dark for them to see anything. They had walked down two floors when they finally found Peter's cell. James looked through the keyhole, and saw Peter sitting against a wall, staring at the ceiling, talking to himself.

James whispered through the keyhole, "Psst!" Peter stood up, bewildered by the sound, shook his head, decided that he had just imagined it after all, and sat back down. James, frustrated, spoke a bit louder, "Peter!"

He stood up again, and asked the darkness in front of him, "Where?"

"Here!" James whispered. "The door!" Hearing them, Alex rushed toward James.

"That's his cell?"

"Yes," James said. "Would you hand me a stick?"

"What are you going to do," Peter and Alex asked at the same time.

James whispered to Alex, "Burn down his door," and explained to Peter the plan.

"But won't the guard demons see the flames and come up here to check," Peter questioned. James and Alex considered the problem quietly. Their cells were on a higher floor, but Peter's cell was lower down.

"Let's do it anyway," James decided. "You must be rescued, and we have to escape."

"Right," Peter said. "Do it." Five minutes later, Peter was already out of his cell, searching for Liliana's cell. After searching through fifteen cells, Alex finally found a cell with one of the quest members in it, but it wasn't Liliana.

When James and Peter arrived to see who was inside, they all gasped, "Marcus!"

Marcus stopped looking out his cell's window and turned around, searching for the source of the sound.

"The door!" Alex whispered.

Marcus went to the door and asked, "What… Who is it?"

"It's us!"

"Who is 'Us?'"

"It's Alex, Peter and James!"

"You?" Marcus sounded very surprised. "How did you get here?"

"We also want to ask the same question," James said before any of the others could react. "But we have to get you out first."

"But how do you do that?"

"We burn the door down, since it's made of wood," Peter said.

"Cool," Marcus said. "But I could do it by myself."

"What? How?" James asked.

"He can control fire, silly," Alex said and picked up a stick from the ground and threw it into Marcus' cell. Very soon, Marcus was also in the corridor, searching for Liliana's cell, when they heard voices behind them.

The four froze.

"What's-" Marcus started, but Alex clamped her hand over his mouth. James slowly turned around but saw nothing.

Then, as they heard some light footsteps, Peter whispered, "They're demons. They must be coming from below. Quickly, hide!" James threw himself onto the floor, and the others did the same. Then suddenly the footsteps stopped. The two demon guards looked down the other end of the corridor and saw two doors on fire.

"What? How?" one of the guards exclaimed.

"A door on fire?" the other guard said. "Someone's been here." They looked down the other end, but fortunately they didn't see James, Peter, Alex and Marcus.

"I'll search the corridor," the first guard decided. "You go down to tell the others." The other guard strode downstairs, further away from the group, while the first guard headed in the opposite direction from them.

Peter whispered, "We have to go down now."

"What about Liliana," asked Alex.

However, Peter said, "It's too risky. We must save ourselves by going down." Alex reluctantly agreed, and they darted for the exit.

They were one floor below when they heard more guards' boots approaching. James pulled the rest to a corner, covered by a shadow, and waited for the guards to pass.

"-it's unusual for someone who's not a demon to venture so deep into our territory," one said.

"They got past the first mountain range and the demons there!" They had already decided that it was not a demon who set the doors on fire.

"It's unusual," another agreed. "But it might be the three that lord Abaddon questioned yesterday evening."

"Could be, but unlikely," a third guard said. "They're just kids."

"They burned the doors down," the first demon spoke. "They're smart."

"Smart, but we'll get them!" They marched past the group, not noticing them, and headed up.

"Whew," Peter said, "that was close." But James was confused by something that the demons said.

"They said, 'It's unusual for an enemy of the demons to venture this far into demon territory.' Is it actually unusual?"

"Of course it is," Peter said. "Normally, we ignore the demons. This is rare."

James nodded. "Let's continue down."

They bolted down the last two floors of the prison and entered the main base. First, they came to a crossroad, but since none of them actually saw the way in, they decided to randomly pick which direction they went, and they went right. After some ten minutes of following the path, they encountered a door, Alex opened it, and found that it led outdoors, onto a bridge that led to another mountain. The freezing cold air whipped at them, and a light rain had started to pour, gradually growing heavier. James looked at the other side of the bridge, and there were some stairs leading down to the forest below. Although they were guarded, James told the others that they had to use the stairs. They concurred and made for the stairs. When they reached them, Alex threw the first guard over the side, while James grabbed another one's dagger and stabbed him in the back with it. Peter kicked another guard's butt, which sent him flying down the stairs, lying dead. Marcus stunned the last guard and cut off the guard's hands with a sword. Then, as the four ran down the stairs, a yell came from behind them, and as they glanced back, a few dozen demons were bolting across the bridge, chasing them.

"Quick!" Marcus and Alex shouted. They reached the bottom of the stairs, grabbed weapons from the defeated guards, and ran into the demons' city.

James pulled the others into a clump of bushes as the guards sprinted by, not noticing them. Then the four of them walked around and found a small clearing surrounded by trees, where they could sit down and talk. James sat down on the wet ground.

"Where do we go now?" Alex asked the others.

"No idea," Peter said. "It's almost impossible to continue through this demon-inhabited city, there are demons *everywhere.*"

"Do we return to the forest? And why did we come to these 'towns' in the first place?" All their heads turned to James, as if they expected him to have an answer.

James grudgingly made a decision and said, "We could continue on to the mountains. This way, we're not fully retreating to the forest or in plain sight of the demons."

"We *would* be in plain sight of the demons," Alex argued. "They have bases all over the mountains. I say that we retreat to the forest." James argued back, but Peter interrupted him, agreeing with Alex and saying that if they stayed there any longer, then they would be discovered because of the noise they were making. Marcus led the group into the forest again, under the cover of tall trees, thick bushes and dense undergrowth.

Fifteen
The Quest Continued

That night, they slept in a tiny clearing until dawn (which was actually only two hours away). They were too scared to make a campfire because the demons might notice the smoke, and they were wet and cold throughout the night. But when dawn came, only a few rays of sun were able to penetrate through the thick, grey clouds, and the rain poured down heavier than ever. The group woke wearily, walked around their tiny 'camp,' and continued their journey around the mountains.

After a while James suddenly asked, "Why are we going around the mountains? Isn't Gremword supposed to be in the middle of the Forest of Demons?" The others thought for a while before answering.

"Maybe we can find a place where there are lesser demons and go inside the mountains!" Peter finally said.

"And do you want to go *inside* the city?" Alex added. James didn't reply to them. After two hours, at midmorning, the rain was still pouring down. Marcus asked them to sit down, rest and have some water perhaps. The rest agreed, and James found a nearby stream to drink from. Thirty minutes later, they got up and continued.

It was now the middle of the afternoon, and the downpour turned into a moderate rain. They were resting again, and in fact James thought that they'd actually had a lucky day - the demons had never noticed them from their hidden bases.

Then, Alex said, "I think after resting, we should go inside the city now." The others looked at her as if she was crazy. Then, James agreed.

"We've stayed outside long enough. Maybe there are less demons in this region. If it doesn't go well, we can always escape."

"Really?" Peter asked.

"Come on," Marcus said. "They're right. We should at least check." Peter followed them up the steep mountain, but they were constantly tripping. They cut themselves several times but finally reached the summit after a hard climb. To their joy, there were less demons living in this area, and James saw why. There was an extremely thick entangle of undergrowth, plants, bushes, moss, and piles of twigs or dirt that was almost impossible to clear. They descended the mountain and arrived at the foot of it. When they looked down from the summit, the nearest house was quite far away, and they didn't speak as they struggled through the undergrowth. Finally at sunset, they reached the first house and decided to camp some hundred metres away to the left of it, just to be safe.

"We've gone quite far today," Marcus said. Alex shook her wet hair out of her face.

"Now we have to think about not letting the demons find us."

After sunset, Marcus suggested that they get food. He and James walked a bit closer to the mountains and searched for small animals, such as squirrels and rabbits. They caught three of these, tied them up and returned to the others, who had already found a stream, a bucket and had brought a bucket of water back. They were sipping it tiredly when Marcus threw the three dead animals onto the floor beside them and sat down.

Peter looked over and said, "I was surprised that there were any animals living in this demon-infested area."

"We found them by a stream," James explained. "The rabbit was drinking from it, and the squirrels were climbing on a tree."

"How will we eat them?" Alex asked. The others didn't know what they would say. "If we cook it, then the fire would surely be seen by the demons. And we shouldn't… eat it raw."

Then, Marcus said, "I could control the fire so that it's low and won't have smoke."

"That'd work," James said, and they built the campfire in the middle of the clearing. Thirty minutes later, they had cooked the meat and eaten it. Then, Peter took the first watch, as the others curled up on the ground. James was asleep before a minute passed, but he dreamed about Hans and Nolan again.

The two demons were on their boat, leaving an island. James could see a patch of islands behind them, and Hans muttered to himself, "The base doesn't seem to be around here, too. Where could it be?"

Nolan sat at the other end of the boat, thinking aloud quietly, "Maybe the base isn't here at all!" The boat was heading straight toward the Kingdom of Alemis. If they didn't see the base along the way, they would go on shore at the Kingdom, maybe get a night or two's sleep and some provisions and continue on the long journey into the demons' territory. As they talked to each other, Nolan caught a glint of light – sunlight reflecting from glass - in the air to the left of them.

"What's that?" he asked.

"What's what?"

"There was a glint of light there, in the middle of the sky." Then, the light appeared again.

"That's weird," Hans said. "Steer the boat there to investigate." Then, they rowed in the direction of the light, their boat suddenly bumped onto an invisible thing, and a secret island appeared, right in front of them, with huge trees and bushes and cliffs winding up, almost touching the sky. "Ah, good," Hans said. "This must be their base." Then James woke up with a start. He was nervous because he knew that his dreams could be true, and if this one *was* true then his…their…base would be located by the demons.

The others listened nervously to James sharing the news the next morning. The rain had stopped.

"So, if they've found our base," Peter said, "then that probably means that they'll be planning to attack it. Gremword will want revenge."

"That means that we have to be quick about finding him and killing him." Marcus said. "Which means that we should continue now. The middle of the Forest of Demons should be in the direction of the house that we found a while back. Get up." They stood up and continued on their way. At midmorning they had reached a second house, and following the second house a few dozen more houses. The four made slow progress here, ducking from bush to bush. Finally, they had passed the row of demonic houses, maybe a village, and continued through the dense undergrowth and thick bushes. Then, suddenly, a spurt of flame shot up into the sky above the clouds in front of them in the distance and then died again.

"What was that?" James asked.

"No idea," Marcus said. "It's quite far away, so we probably don't have to worry about it."

When the sun reached its zenith, the group sat down and rested. The day was going perfectly well - they had not even been spotted once. They walked a few metres to the right of them, and since they hadn't brought the bucket of water with them, they set out to find a stream. It was a while before James realised that they hadn't brought their weapons with them.

"But it's too late to go back and get them now," Alex said. "That way we'll spend this whole day doing nothing."

"Then how will we get new weapons?"

"We'll worry about that later. Now, we must get water, and hopefully, food." They found a nearby stream to drink and wash their faces in, and some berries.

As they sat down and ate them, they heard some footsteps and Peter tackled Alex into a bush. James and Marcus scrambled into the dense undergrowth just as three demons appeared in the small, cleared space.

"That's odd," one said. "I never remembered a cleared space here."

"Told you," a second demon said, "I heard something."

"Come on, guys," the third demon said. "The cleared space could've been made by the downpour yesterday. And that something that you heard could've been a squirrel or a bird."

"No," the second one said. "It didn't sound like a squirrel or a bird. More like…a demon, or a human, or even worse…"

"What?" the third demon asked. "Even worse what?"

The second demon said, "Even worse, an enemy of the demons." Without them seeing, the first demon had quietly slipped away, and was not in this area anymore. Then, James and Peter heard branches rustling behind them and decided to run. A millisecond later, a pair of hands lunged through the bushes behind them, and the four escaped only just in time.

"You won't get away after invading our territory!" a voice growled, and a demon leaped through the bushes.

Thinking that there were a lot of pursuers behind, the group ran through the trees. They had been fleeing from their pursuer for two minutes when James realised that there was only one pursuer. Suddenly, he skidded to a stop and punched the demon in the face, and with the force of the punch and the demon's speed he managed to defeat him, only to see that there were more demons behind, there were two or three more. But, noticing that James was behind them, the rest of them turned and faced the demons. The first of them swung an axe, and almost hit James's head, but he ducked, picked up the fallen demon's sword and counterattacked. It struck the demon in his chest, and then he fell. The two remaining demons dodged Alex and Peter's attacks, but Marcus kicked a demon in the guts, and he staggered back. One demon came at Alex with a killing strike, but she summoned wind and blew the weapon away. Then, Peter picked up a dagger, threw it, and struck a demon full in the face. But the last demon was quicker than they thought. He swiped twice at Marcus' legs and came up with a strike in James' chest. Twelve milliseconds later, his sword was coming at Alex's head, and she knew that she would not be able to dodge quickly enough. Without thinking, she raised her wrist just in time to stop it from beheading her, but instead it wounded her severely in the arm. With a roar of anger and pain, she punched the demon in the cheeks with her good arm, just as James leaped onto the demon, brought him down to the ground and sliced off his feet and hands. With a last bellow, the demon died.

But the sound of the fighting caused more demons to come over and see what was happening in their neighbourhood. James, Peter, Alex and Marcus ran away just in time as a crowd of them filed in. When they couldn't hear the demons behind them anymore, they sat down in a small clearing and rested for a while.

"Are you okay?" Peter asked, looking at the slash in James's chest as it bled.

James glanced at the blood flowing from Alex's forearm, nodded and said, "Cover it up, Alex."

She looked at James and asked, "Why?" James pretended that he didn't hear her.

Marcus was squatting on the edge of the clearing, keeping watch, but then he suddenly said, "They're coming. There are lots of them; the whole 'town,' maybe."

"So, we run?" Peter asked.

"No," Marcus said. "I'm done with running away. There is a 'town' of them, but most of them aren't soldiers, just women, old people and children. We could fight them."

"Marcus, I don't think we should fight women, old people and children."

"Why not? They're demons." Then, behind them, they heard the crowd of demons gasp at the sight of the three dead demons. Then, the underbrush behind them exploded as the demons ran into the clearing, angry because of the fallen demons and seeing the group.

A split second later, the four children reacted to the demons' attack. They turned around, and saw a few dozen demons armed with broomsticks, daggers and poles. Demons weren't ugly and they looked like normal humans, but them charging at the group was a terrifying sight. Then, as the four attacked, the demons waved their weapons, shouting and screaming. James kicked a demon in the stomach, grabbed his staff and ran up a tree. Alex began kicking and punching demons, summoning wind and knocking them down. Peter grabbed a frying pan from one demon, slapped her on the head and fought other demons the same way. Each of Marcus's kicks that struck home put a wound on a demon. But, as they fought, more demons arrived as there was more noise, and seeing the fallen demons they joined in the attack. James suddenly found himself fighting a strong, burly male with only a dagger, for his staff was grabbed away. The demon landed a blow on his face, and as James's dagger found his thigh the demon roared and kicked him. Peter and Alex found themselves back-to-back, surrounded by demons. Marcus was about to be overrun by three demon soldiers armed with spear-axes, and then they were joined by a few others, when James leaped over and saved him.

"Thanks," Marcus muttered.

"Don't thank me," James said as he blocked another stab.

They fought for almost three quarters of an hour, when the demons were all defeated (meaning that the surviving ones ran away). Peter urged them to run, because another crowd of demons might return and land them back in big trouble. When they were far enough from the demons, they lay down on the floor in exhaustion. Then, after a few minutes, they sat up and nursed their wounds. They had only won because the demons weren't *proper* soldiers and would have been turned into the mincemeat if it wasn't for their supreme reaction skills. As they sat down, animals walked around them, and Peter suddenly heard a stream gurgling not far from them. He walked over to get water, while the rest lay down and stretched. For a long time nobody talked, and James broke the silence.

"Where do we go next?" Marcus pointed behind him.

"That direction. But we can't keep on getting into fights like that."

"It was your idea," Alex said.

"*Was* my idea," Marcus said, "but not my idea now." They were quiet then until Peter returned with some water and fish to eat. Alex skinned the fish; Marcus cooked it, and they ate the fish. After that, they got up, and continued on their journey, until sunset, when they stopped by a river.

They walked until their ankles hurt and feet were sore. Marcus told them to stop at sunset, because he couldn't go on anymore. The rest agreed and they rested until the sun was fully down, when they used the darkness and shadows to creep across the village. Then they walked for an hour or two, when they finally curled up and slept. James took the first watch, while the others slept. A few hours later, Marcus woke up and took the second watch, and James went to sleep. This time, he dreamed of Hans and Nolan again, but this time they were in a forest, and James recognised it - The Forest of Demons.

They were driving in Nolan's SUV parallel to a river, but the sailors were nowhere to be seen.

"Not far now," said Nolan. "It's just over those next mountains, and a hundred and one kilometres southwest."

"And when Lord Gremword hears the news, he'll send an army to conquer them, and then demons shall rule the world!" Hans smiled.

"Of course! But most importantly, our lord shall be extremely pleased with us for finding the island, and we shall have a warm welcome." They drove on for a few kilometres, until they reached the mountains, where they went upward, and their car's wheels shifted, so that they could ascend more easily. They were still following the river, which had turned into a stream. Then, they finally reached a cave, where there was a demon guard post.

Fifteen demons advanced out of the post, when Hans said, "We have returned after a mission for Lord Gremword, having successfully found the enemy training base for their children."

The demon guards surrounded their car, and their officer asked, "Password, and your identity?"

"124783, and there is no need for my identity, I suppose. Let us in!" The officer nodded, the guards returned to their post and Hans and Nolan drove past.

James woke up in the bushes that they were sleeping in and sat up. He looked around and saw the others lying around them. But when he looked around the trees, he spotted an orange thing crouching in the undergrowth a few metres away. Because he wasn't sure what it was, he advanced to try to see what the orange shape was. Suddenly, the undergrowth exploded, and a large, fearsome tiger pounced out of the trees. Its roar was deafening, but with one strike James had severed one of its paws from its body. However, the furious beast had still landed on James and was scratching angrily at his chest. James rolled over, stabbed the tiger's stomach and stood up. He hurled his dagger into the tiger's forehead, and it collapsed, dead. The noise had woken Peter.

"What was that?" he asked.

"Tiger," James said. "It was in the bushes over there, and it jumped onto me."

"Has it wounded you?" James sat down without speaking.

After twenty minutes, the others had woken up, and they decided to move on.

"In my dream, Hans and Nolan mentioned that Gremword was one hundred kilometres southwest of the mountains."

"So, we've been heading in completely the opposite direction," Marcus said.

"Not completely," Peter insisted. "It should be directly south of us now."

"Duck!" Alex suddenly hissed, and they leaped into a clump of bushes. Two demons went past.

"What was that sound?" one said.

"Nothing," the other one comforted the first demon. "Probably an animal." Then the two walked on. After a few minutes, another five demons passed by, and they had to sidestep into the undergrowth once more.

"These demons are annoying," Alex said, as they cautiously rose and moved on. "We always have to duck and move silently, and we never know when they'll suddenly come out."

"They *are* always slowing us down," Peter said. "So, why don't we blend into the demon population?"

"How?" James, Alex and Marcus didn't see how they could do that either.

"We could basically steal some demons' clothes, and pretend to be demons," Peter said.

"You're mad," Alex said.

"But it's a good plan, it would save a lot of time," James said.

"We could do it," Marcus uttered.

"Let's do it now." James pointed to a small cabin around fifty metres away from them. "Let's steal from that one. Small houses are best, as we could make a quick escape."

"Sure," Peter said.

"Alex and Marcus, wait on the outside, Peter, stay at the doorway, and I will get the clothes," James ordered. Although he wasn't the leader of the group, the others did what he said. He crept into the house, heard snoring from inside a bedroom, and saw some clothes hanging from a line on the ceiling. There were cloaks, shirts, pants and shoes. James quietly and slowly took them, making the least noise, and walked out again, joining the others. Covered by the shadow of the trees, they put on their newly stolen clothes, and continued their journey, but with a tiny bit more confidence.

Sixteen
Gremword's Palace

They had encountered seventeen demons on the first day wearing their demons' clothes, and every time they met one, they nodded and moved on.

In the afternoon, Peter took off his cloak and said, "That was quite a good idea."

"Yeah." The others agreed. They were all getting quite confident.

"I'm thinking about going to an inn and getting a proper meal and sleeping on a bed," Marcus said. All they had been eating was rabbits, squirrels and wild berries.

"But the demons only have to glance at us to see that we're not demons. They might come into our rooms at night when we're sleeping, or look at us when we're eating. Going to an inn is far too dangerous," James scolded. "We should just keep going as we are now."

After another two hours, the sun had begun to set. The group decided to sleep in the forest, far from houses.

"Just in case someone comes along and sees us," James explained. "We should also get some food before dark." Alex threw a knife and killed a rabbit and used her wind powers to blow it into the air. The rabbit landed on her hands, and she swiftly skinned and chopped it up in even slices. The whole sequence took around forty seconds. Marcus grabbed two sticks, created two torches and made a campfire in twenty seconds. James summoned four balls of water and placed it in front of each of his friends in ten seconds. Peter grabbed a few leaves, placed them on the fire, and put the rabbit on the leaves. After a few minutes, the meat was cooked thoroughly, and they ate all of it.

Marcus, who had already finished his portion, asked, "So do we sleep now?"

"What do you think? Of course!"

"I'll take the first watch," Peter volunteered. The rest fell asleep immediately.

In his dream, James saw Hans and Nolan again, but this time they were walking, not driving. They stopped right beside two enormous waterfalls, and Hans spoke, "124783." Thirty demons stepped out of secret entrances behind the waterfalls.

Their officer said, "Hans and Nolan. Returning from a mission for Lord Gremword. Yes, guard post 378 sent a message ahead by telephone. The lord also knows. Please enter." The officer bowed and the guards parted, gesturing for the two to pass. Hans and Nolan both entered the waterfall on the right, but as they went through, they seemed to disappear, vanish.

A few seconds later, James's dream changed. Hans and Nolan suddenly appeared on the end of a long, straight corridor with a red-and-yellow carpet, and lined with dim lights. Behind them, a door seemed to hang open, facing the waterfall. The two men began to walk. As they reached the very end of the corridor, they both said, "387421." The walls swung open, revealing three more corridors of the same length, but decorated more beautifully. They both entered the corridor straight ahead, which split into two corridors. They followed the corridor on the right, which curved, and Hans and Nolan found themselves facing a large steel gate. They both flicked their fingers, the gates opened, and they entered Gremword's huge courtyard. James woke, and realised that he wasn't there with the demons, which was a relief.

When James woke, everyone was already up. Peter and Marcus were eating the remaining scraps of yesterday's rabbit for breakfast, while Alex, who was not hungry, sipped at a bit of the water that James had summoned.

When James sat up, Alex said, "Well, he's up." The others looked at James.

"How long have you all been up?" he asked.

"One hour at least," Peter replied. "I did a bit of exploring after sunrise, and I found two enormous waterfalls directly south of here, three kilometres away. The strange thing was, one of them seemed to glow dimly, just a bit, and I was afraid to go in. So, I came back, told everyone else about it, and we decided to wait for you to get up. We could have a basic breakfast, and we didn't want you to wake up finding that we were gone. And," he added, "you could have some breakfast first. Drink some water."

James agreed to Peter's requests, and when he finished the bit of rabbit, he said to the others, "Well, let's go. If we linger around, we'll never find Gremword's palace."

Although the group had their demons' clothes on (which were blown away a bit at night but were quickly recovered), they still kept close to the useful shelter and shadows of the forest. A drizzle had started when they had arrived at the waterfalls.

Peter said, "These are the waterfalls that I was talking about. Maybe I should-"

"Wait," James interrupted, suddenly remembering his dream. "Last night I dreamed about Hans and Nolan entering their ruler's base. It was behind a waterfall, and it was identical to these two! Except...they didn't glow."

The others were already very interested in the demon lord's palace, and Alex asked, "What security systems does it have?"

"Wait," James said, "I'm not even sure that this is the correct waterfall. The demons only had to say the password twice, but maybe there's a sensor which detects if we're demons or not, and more challenges for non-demons."

"Anyway, we should try it. And James, do you recall the password, if there is one?"

James thought for a few minutes, and said, "1247… and something. It's probably 8…124783! The password is 124783."

"Great!" Peter exclaimed. "Now, when do we say the password?"

"When we enter the waterfall on the right, say the password. We would appear inside a corridor, and then I'll tell you what to do next. And did we bring our weapons?"

"I did," Marcus said. "Let's go now." They made a run for the waterfall.

As they ran towards the waterfall, demons materialised out of the opposite one, and ran toward them, holding weapons and screaming.

"Quick!" Alex urged. They dove into the waterfall, shouting, "124783," and closing their mouths before the water could flow in.

A second later, they appeared in the corridor, and James explained to them as they darted down the corridor, "When we get to the end of the corridor, shout, '387421,' and turn right!"

"This *is* Gremword's palace and base, we've found it," Marcus gasped as they turned a corner.

Peter heard a splashing sound behind them, saw some demon guards and shouted, "James!" James turned around and forced the water to hold back the demons. However, that made him a bit tired, and he had to be supported by Alex in order not to fall. They rushed on towards the gate, but then suddenly a tripwire appeared in front of their ankles. The ground disappeared right in front of them, and although Alex desperately gave them a little boost with wind they still fell. Peter attempted to gather the dust on the rim and the bottom of the pit without success. Then, Marcus accidentally set fire to the others' clothes.

"Marcus!" Alex yelled in fear, anger and pain, but they levitated for a second, which allowed James to douse the fire and summon water to push them up. They crumpled on the ground, exhausted, but Peter rolled, stood up and pulled the others up. They stood up and continued their run towards the gate.

When they reached the gate, Peter knelt down so that Alex could use his back as a ramp and somersault over. Then, they helped Marcus and James up, and Peter went last. As they landed on the ground, the people wandering around in Gremword's courtyard stared at them, and drew their weapons, seeing that they were not demons. The group drew their own weapons, and after five minutes twenty demons were wiped out. Noticing a gap in the demons' attack, the group ran through it and found themselves facing Gremword's palace.

The palace was magnificent, but it was impossible to describe it as beautiful. Tourmaline walls rose up high above the ground, while gloomy obsidian towers were lined with bronze and tungsten. Dim lamps hung above stained windows, where shadows lingered creepily. The plants and mahogany trees that decorated the gardens were dark and overgrown as if Gremword was too lazy to bother with these types of things. Basalt pillars supported the entrance gate and several other platforms on the walls.

Forty of the demonic royal guards noticed them and ran to assault them, brandishing weapons and firing arrows.

"Spread out!" James called. The rest did that, splitting into two groups. James was with Peter. As they were only seven metres away from the royal guards, they all ducked and ran in opposite directions. "Confuse them and get behind the demon ranks!" Alex used a demon's shoulder as a support, and side-vaulted over him. James kicked one of them and somersaulted over the demon ranks. Peter and Marcus met in the middle, wounded two demons, leaving a wide gap in between the other demons. Then, they ran for the door, and the last two demon guards fled.

"You'll never get in that door!" one demon laughed. But it turned out that they didn't use the door. They climbed up some pillars to a second-floor window, and slipped in.

The place they had slipped into was a security vault. Next, Alex opened the door, and they all ran outside, to find themselves facing three elegantly dressed demons, which appeared to be Gremword's advisor and two guests. Even demons are civilised enough to honour guests, but once the advisor saw the four outsiders, he drew his sword and attacked. After hesitating for a split second, the guests also stepped forward to assault them, but suddenly they found Peter and James were already behind them. The demons barely had time to gasp before James beheaded one guest, Marcus disarmed the advisor, and Alex stunned a female guest. Then, Peter and Marcus were locked in a fierce duel with the advisor, who was a surprisingly good swordsman. But then, Alex and James joined in, and he was finally overcome. After the group dragged the defeated demons to a corner, they ran around the corner, nearly being seen by another demon.

They had run for about ten minutes before Peter realised something and asked, "Wait. We need a plan, and we don't even know where Gremword is. I mean, we don't know which part of this palace Gremword is in. Just running around is pointless."

"We need a plan," Alex agreed. "Maybe we could split up?"

"No, that would be too risky," James contended. "We'd better stay together, and there needs to be a room large enough for Gremword to be in there. Maybe we could go to the dining hall?"

"But we don't know where the dining hall is."

"It's probably at the centre of the palace. Anyway, let's go there," Marcus said. They started heading to the centre of the palace. They went downstairs and saw a strange sight: A few tunnels heading down, and staircases that shifted every few minutes. Although they didn't know that Gremword lived underground, and that they could go underground through the tunnels. "Come on," James said, "It's not here; let's try somewhere else."

After a few minutes, they had found the centre of the palace, and an enormous, beautifully decorated dining hall. The water demons' dining hall at the bottom of the ocean was nothing compared to this; this dining hall was full of golden chairs, silver tables and walls full of expensive paintings and tables full of diamond plates and crystals. The demon lord was not here, but who *was* here were Gremword's top advisors and generals, his best spies, and some other trusted people dining and chatting. At once, their heads all turned toward the door that James had just opened.

"Who's that?" one general asked.

"They're not demons," another general said. "Why are you here," he asked threateningly as he advanced, hand balanced on his sword. He was a frightening sight, a two-metre-tall, muscular man.

"Um…" James said and then came up with an idea. "I was delivering a message for Lord Gremword."

"So, who told you to do that?"

"General Kolvien told me to tell Lord Gremword that-," James said.

"You are not a demon." The general who spoke first raised his voice. "I, Kolvien, never use non-demons. And I recognize you. You were the person whom I imprisoned, and you and your ruddy friends have escaped. But, this time, you shall be caught and never released!"

As James had expected, the demons quickly leapt forward and began attacking him.

"Run!" he shouted, and they all bolted out of the hall, followed by the demons. But fortunately, they had managed to catch the demons by surprise as Alex threw her weapon behind her, and they all leaped into a small room to their left. James kicked the door shut, and they lay on the floor, panting. He heard the demons rush past. Peter opened the door by a centimetre, and peeked out, seeing that no one was there, and motioned to his friends that it was clear. One by one, they crawled out and also saw that no one was there.

"So, now that we saw that Gremword wasn't in the dining hall," Alex said, "where do we search next?"

"Maybe he's in one of the tunnels we saw earlier when we were looking for the dining hall," Marcus suggested.

"Why do you think *that* would be where Gremword is?"

"He's a snake," Marcus said. "He's big. Underground, there's a lot of space, and snakes also live underground."

"Good idea," James said. "It's probably the next right turn." Then they descended into the darkness of the tunnels. Meanwhile, the generals had grabbed the nearest telephone and sent a message to Gremword, saying that Alex, Peter and James had entered his palace. Gremword was angry that the generals had not captured them, but he didn't message the generals.

When they reached the bottom of the staircase (which was amazingly grand, despite the fact that it was made of stone and dirt), they found themselves facing a crossroad of four tunnels, all decorated amazingly. One of them had a blue carpet, one a yellow carpet, one a red carpet and the one leading straight ahead had no carpet, but there were long, golden tables stretching to the end of the corridor. A chandelier made of black onyx hung on the ceiling, and beside it were two words printed perfectly in solid diamond: THRONE ROOM. The group walked on, realising that the throne room must be at the end of this corridor. Indeed, there was a door made of a mixture of some of the most precious and rare stones and metals at the end of the corridor.

"Ready?" James whispered. The others nodded. And then they opened the door.

Seventeen
The Triumph

The guards heard footsteps outside the door and a voice whispering, "Ready?" before Gremword did. Then as the door creaked open, Gremword slithered across the eighty-metre-long, twenty-metre-wide, ten-metre-tall room, or more correctly, hall. He had just recognised who they were, as one of the generals had alerted him.

"WHAT ARE YOU DOING IN MY PALACE?" he roared. James said nothing. Instead, he sprinted forward, and as the guards closed in the others formed a small triangle behind him. But with one blast of Gremword's fire, the group were forced to roll towards the exit. Gremword and four dozen guards advanced on them, forcing them towards an exit. Fighting in the open would be easier, Gremword thought, as he backed the intruders down a corridor. But unexpectedly, Alex suddenly leaped into the air and landed on Gremword's shoulders. But when she drove her knife into Gremword's body, she found that the gap between his scales were too thin.

"Ha!" Gremword shouted. "I am invincible!" Then, arms sprouted out of his shoulders, each holding a glowing, magical, sharp, diamond sword. Next, another pair of arms grew straight below the first pair. Both of these arms held spear-axes. He swung the spears at James and Peter as they tried to get close to Gremword, but then suddenly his sword arms drove the weapons into the ground right beside them. Then, his tail grabbed hold of Marcus and would have killed him, if it was not for Alex, who kicked Gremword and got his attention.

"WHAT THE-" Gremword roared deafeningly. Then, he hurled Marcus onto the floor, while the Generals Avexor and Santlus easily held back James, Peter and Alex.

"We must all fight Gremword together," Peter shouted over the din of battle. But then, Gremword spat venom on the ground, and attacked with all four of his arms. After twenty minutes, they were forced to flee to ground level.

Outside, there was a thunderstorm brewing. The rain swiftly soaked the surrounding area, plants, grass, and buildings, and Gremword's generals sprinted out of the exit. Then, the ground rumbled beneath the group's feet, and they barely had time to jump away before Gremword broke through the ground, causing dirt and rocks to fly everywhere. As he came out of the gaping hole in the ground, James sprinted towards him, but Gremword suddenly sprouted a new pair of arms, holding one machine gun with a hundred and twenty bullets and one custom rifle with fifty bullets. He emptied out the machine gun at James and Alex, peppering the ground with holes, and took a few shots at the air with the assault rifle at the same time. Then, as Peter and Marcus attempted to attack Gremword from both sides, the machine gun suddenly ran out of ammunition. However, Gremword's reactions were quick, and he swung his spear-axes, and his archers also shot a few deadly, poisoned arrows at James, but only one of them hit him - on the tip of his shoe. Then, Gremword held out his assault rifle, and shot ten rounds at Alex, who dodged all of them, but they slowed her down and made her back away. At the same time, Peter and Marcus attempted to avoid Gremword's blows but were also taking some wounds.

Unexpectedly, Gremword's generals took out black automatic pistols and fired them, making a hail of yellow bullets speed towards the children, slowing them down.

"We need to surround Gremword!" James shouted as he rolled on the ground to avoid a bullet. Then, he somersaulted over another one, landing on his back. He punched a demon officer, which caused him to drop his pistol, but another soldier picked it up and fired a shot at James. However, he was too quick and was already on top of the soldier's head before he knew it. As they wrestled for the gun, another general shot at James, but instead he hit the soldier that James was fighting with. James took the gun and saw Peter struggling with General Vaughn, so he tossed the weapon to Peter, who shot the general straight away. But Vaughn had deflected the missile with his katana and brought the sword down towards Peter. However, Peter summoned a sandstorm, and the full force of the sand slammed into Vaughn. He stumbled and was blinded for a few seconds. James nodded at his friend and rushed off.

Alex and Marcus were on the other side of the battlefield, battling Gremword. However, the lord of the demons seemed to be invulnerable, and as they danced around trying to avoid his bullets and weapons, Gremword knew that he was only playing with them. It was extremely easy to keep them at bay. But James arrived and snuck up behind Gremword. At the last second, he jumped up, scuttled on top Gremword's left shoulder, and rolled over his head. James landed on top of the assault rifle and was preparing to jerk it out of Gremword's grip when the huge snake's spear axe came slicing through the air, and James had to leap onto the ground to avoid it. Marcus then set his dagger on fire and almost wounded Gremword, but sadly the hopeless blade shattered against the strong scales. Weaponless, Marcus rolled on the muddy grass to prevent Gremword from launching an accurate blow at him, and Alex and

James attacked Gremword from his left-hand side. Peter then joined them, vaulting over a guard. Together, they attacked the demon-lord, James and Alex climbing to his head, Peter attacking the sword arms, Marcus preventing the generals from getting near. As they attempted to kill Gremword, the demonic generals closed in. With a flick of his tail, Gremword sent all the kids flying away from him. He laughed loudly.

James flew through the air and landed on a patch of grass behind a few soldiers. As he got up, he caught a highly ranked demon soldier by surprise and cut off one of his hands. That officer dropped his assault rifle, and as James picked it up, he fired three shots at Gremword. Although he didn't bleed, one of Gremword's scales on the shoulder of one of his arms bent on the first bullet. The second and third bullets shattered that small scale. Peter noticed the shattered scale and saw the demon lord's skin underneath. At the same time, Gremword roared and directed the tip of his tail at Marcus, who was duelling General Santlus, and hadn't seen the venom coming. In a few seconds, his screaming body was on fire, and the venom had consumed it. The demons, seeing this, cheered loudly, while Alex, Peter and James shouted, "NO!"

Gremword attacked just as they were rushing towards the deceased body of Marcus. He aimed his gun at them and shot a bullet. At the last second, James turned around, saw the yellow projectile of death, and pushed the others onto the ground. Then, Gremword's swords came at them like a leopard's claws, but somehow James managed to parry and block every attack. But Gremword's hands holding the spear-axes joined in the attack, and Peter came to James's defence. Suddenly, James slipped away and leaped on top of Gremword. Then, he scrambled up his arm, and using the other arms like ladders he finally managed to plunge a dagger inside the hole made by his stolen assault rifle.

Gremword roared in anger and pain. Blood ran out of his shoulder, and he dropped his weapons. Alex picked up the rifle and Peter held one of the magical diamond swords. Then, Alex fired the gun multiple times at Gremword, but it was James who delivered the killing blow. As Peter used his new sword to deflect Gremword's fire, James turned the rifle on automatic, and let it spit out twenty bullets at the lord of the demons. Then, he backflipped in the air, and landed on his feet, watching Gremword's massive body collapse. Then immediately he ran towards Marcus and picked his body up from the ground. His generals watched in shock as their leader died, but their shock soon turned into anger. With a shout, they advanced on James, Peter and Alex, cornering them.

"Run!" Alex screamed as she hacked her way through the crowd. James looked at the demon generals, hesitated and lifted Marcus up, carrying him toward his friends. When they escaped from the demon generals, they ran for the forest.

Eighteen
Demon's Revenge Foiled

When the generals were out of sight, they sat down in a clump of bushes and panted.

"I can't believe we actually did it," Peter panted. "That was amazing!"

"Not too amazing," Alex said. "Marcus was sacrificed."

"We managed to defeat Gremword!"

"And now we have to find our way back. We must find the yachts that we left on the beach and sail them back to the island base. We don't even know exactly where we left the yachts, or where the base is! We are in so much trouble now."

"We must believe that we can get back," James said. "Now, we went southwest to get here, which means that we must go northeast. The sun is setting in that direction, meaning that northeast is in that-" James points to a high cliff- "direction-"

"Meaning that we must climb that damned cliff," Alex said. "Great. Now, how in the world do we climb that? It's probably nearly twice the height of that climbing wall we used to train on."

"We can go around it," Peter pointed out. After Alex reluctantly followed, they began the long trip around the cliff.

At the same time, the demons were raging over their defeat.

"IT'S YOU STUPID FIFTEEN IDIOTS' FAULT!" General Avexor roared at one of his special melee attack squads. "YOU DUMMIES COULD HAVE RUSHED FORWARD TOGETHER IN THE PHALANX

FORMATION THAT YOU'VE TRAINED A MILLION TIMES IN, INSTEAD OF JUST ATTACKING WILDLY BY YOURSELVES!" Santlus was also bellowing at some of his men.

"Why," he said, "didn't you attack ferociously? Our lord was under attack!" Officer Steiner was punishing the thirty or so troopers that he had under his control, giving them only half-rations for dinner.

"Only ten minutes for dinner. After dinner, one hundred push-ups, a hundred sit-ups, do the obstacle course ten times, run five kilometres, and repeat until bedtime at ten!" Legate Staunton just passed by.

"Steiner," he said, "that is too little. My troops do more than that every day! You are far too soft on them."

"Fine!" Steiner then told his troops to go to the punishing room. When they were gone, he told the master of the punishment room by telephone to punish the new arrivals. The master agreed, as he loved punishing people.

A few hours later, some of the demon generals had calmed down a bit.

"We must have revenge on those who killed our lord," General Zetrov said. "A trap - something they won't expect would be perfect."

"But to lay a trap for them, dear Zetrov," Vaughn said, "we must know where they are and where they are heading. If we don't, won't it be madness?"

"Oh!" Another general named Gretzky suddenly noticed something. "We could launch an invasion of their base. Hans and Nolan told us all we had to know."

"We need a plan first," Staunton said. "Some tactics. Their base is on an island with tall cliffs, and we need to break in."

"Whoever said that? Siege it! Fire cannons and set off bombs! Surround it, and when there are enough holes, storm in! Simple is best."

"No," Staunton said, "you forgot the provisions, and equipment. We also need tents and to retreat out of sight after the first attack. Call in the royal strategist!" A few minutes later, the strategist, Bukvadom, entered the dining hall with his assistant Ivicses.

"So, you are planning to conquer an island," Bukvadom said, after the generals had explained what they had to do. "Surrounded by tall cliffs. You want to bomb it."

"Yes," Avexor said impatiently. "Now, you are a strategist. Tell us exactly how to do that."

"Firstly," Bukvadom said, "it must be as swift as possible, in order for you to not take too many provisions. Bombing it is a good idea, as scaling the cliffs would take too long. Normally, bombing it would take around one or two days. One question. How many men do you want to take? Consider this: With too many men there will not be enough provisions, but with too few men you would not be able to storm it."

Zetrov thought for a moment, and decided, "Around fifteen thousand."

"That is too many," Bokvadom said. "I was thinking more about two thousand and three hundred infantry and five hundred bowmen. This number is enough to storm a medium-sized castle, if used correctly. Fifteen thousand? I would use that on the Fesittes' palace."

"Fine," Zetrov complained. "Then, two thousand, five hundred and fifty infantry and four hundred and fifty archers. How do we transport the provisions?"

"Bring extra ships for them. Take the provisions from one ship to another with cranes, and take enough to feed seventy percent of your troops, but enough armour for all of them. You can steal from the island-base. Use three large battleships, six medium ones and twelve small ones to surround it, and once you make a landing immediately attack. The landing must be swift, and when you storm it only use three-quarters of your troops. Fresh soldiers might be needed. You can even bomb from afar by placing catapults on the ships. It is a good idea to connect the ships; if one of the ships falls, the other ships would pull it back up. Now, I hope that is enough information for you, and I must leave." Bukvadom left the hall with Ivicses following him.

Three hours later, Peter found a less steep mountain trail leading up towards the summit.

"I found a good way up," he called, and seconds later the others were all walking up the trail. After forty-five minutes of walking, they arrived at a hidden valley between two enormous, tree-covered hills.

"Be careful in this valley," James warned. "It's a great ambush point, and the attackers might hide in the trees." Actually, a few dozen demons were hiding in the trees. Steiner, who was bringing some troops to the seaside, had seen Peter on the mountain trail a few minutes ago, and was now lying in ambush with twenty archers ready to fire, ten on each side. Behind the archers were two giant ballistae, which were already loaded and ready with heavy boulders in the place of arrows. When James got to the middle of the valley, two boulders the size of a human were launched into the sky, and thirty arrows swiftly sped toward them. Five seconds later, soldiers rushed out of the trees, forming a spiked wall of spears and shields.

"Run!" James yelled.

"There's nowhere to escape, we're trapped!" Alex shouted back. The demons easily surrounded them.

"I still have Gremword's sword," Peter said. "And you both have rifles. Kill them!" Alex turned her rifle on automatic, and the bullets spat out at the demons, making holes in the enemies' shields. Peter wielded his sword and the air around it began to catch fire. James killed one quarter of all the demons with his gun and his dagger, finally allowing them all to escape into the woods. The demons chased after them for a while, led by an officer, but James and Alex killed him. As soon as their officer died, the demons scattered and fled.

When it was nearly noon, they all collapsed onto the ground in exhaustion.

"Let's rest here until afternoon," Alex said. "I'm too tired to go on, and besides, there are no demon houses in this area. The mountain range seems to be quite close."

"We've only come halfway to the mountains, but we must rest."

"We can continue after we eat something," Peter said. "I'm starving, but there's nothing around."

"I'll sleep for now," James decided. "Wake me up when it's the afternoon or when someone attacks." Then he fell asleep almost instantly.

The demons were beginning to move out of the palace. Thousands of them rode in the direction of the sea, where the demons' ports were located. They would take some provisions from Officer Avlogz' port, load them onto his battleships, and head out for the island-base.

"Up ahead we'll be crossing the borders of our territory," Avexor said. "Men, Treslov defence formation, you never know if there's someone hiding. Plus, Steiner got killed or something, so we must be careful too."

"Don't worry," Santlus assured him, "we got hundreds and hundreds of men. Steiner got, what, like seven, eight?"

"But still it's dangerous," Avexor replied.

"Alright," Santlus said. "Okay."

"When will we camp? It's night already."

"Hey, we only started after dinner."

Then, as one of their soldiers looked at him, Avexor boomed, "Continue! I never told you to stop."

"Anyways," Zetrov joined in their conversation, "where is their base? Gremword didn't tell us."

"It's northeast of Avlogz' base," Santlus explained. "Maybe a little more east than north."

"We can use catapults to bomb them, and then storm in," Zetrov said. "But is just storming a good idea?"

"Relax," Santlus comforted him, "simple is best! We'll take the island easily."

James saw and heard this whole conversation in his dream. He was quite nervous about the invasion of the base. Would they be able to hold back the demons? Because of his worriment and fear, he started to toss and turn in his sleep. What would happen? Would it be the end of their base? James noticed that the demons began talking again.

A soldier who looked like a scout rushed in front of Zetrov, kneeled down and reported, "The ground ahead is impassable. There is a swamp two kilometres ahead, followed and surrounded by thick trees. To the northeast of that area, one part of the forest is full of broken trees, with a large amount of thorn bushes and undergrowth."

"What now?" Zetrov asked. "Do we take the Frisgarl mountain pass in the southeast? Although it is far, we'd never get so many horsemen over the mountain if we don't use a mountain pass. But that is a great ambush point."

"As I have just told you, relax," Santlus said. "What could possibly go wrong?" It turned out that they *were* ambushed in that exact mountain pass.

James woke at dawn, but Peter and Alex were both already up.

"He's up," Alex told Peter sleepily.

"How long have you two been up?" James asked.

"I've made breakfast. About twenty minutes or so," Peter said, holding up one third of a cooked rabbit by the tail. "We've both eaten." After James had finished his meal, he suddenly remembered his dream.

"Peter," he said.

"Huh?"

"I dreamed of the demons planning to besiege the – our – island-base. Hans has informed them about its whereabouts, and they are already on the move."

"That's bad," Alex seemed extremely worried. "Is there any way we could stop them, or do you know anything else?"

"They're going southeast from their location to the Frisgarl mountain pass because the land in front of them is rough."

"Well, we can't make use of that."

"Wait!" Peter exclaimed. "We could ambush them! In the Frisgarl mountain pass, we could easily hold them off, because mountain passes are narrow. It'll be like fighting only five demons!"

"Good point! Let's go there."

"But where," James asked, "is the Frisgarl mountain pass even located? Is it far from us?"

"It is almost completely east of Gremword's palace, but a little bit south." Peter said. "We could reach it by noon, I think."

"Where did you learn this?"

"When I was young, before I was sent to the island-base, in my desert village, I learned a bit of geography, and I still remember part of it."

"You've got a good memory."

"Now let's go there, we're just wasting time chatting."

Around noon, they had made it to the mountain pass. Alex heard the faint sound of beating hooves.

"Is that them?"

"Guess so."

"They're cavalry. How will we stop them if they charge?"

"We'll hold them off, don't worry," James tried to reassure her without sounding fearful himself. "They're still a few thousand metres away."

"A few kilometres away? They'll be here in minutes," Peter said. "We need to spring a trap for them."

"What type of trap? We only have minutes to prepare."

"Maybe a pit in the snow?"

"That would take too long. I say that we just, like, fight them, or maybe use the guns to kill them from the trees or something."

"Okay. Let's do it," James agreed. "You two hide in the trees and fire at them with your guns. I'll fight them with Gremword's swords."

"You also come into the trees."

"No. If we only fire from the trees, they might overcome us, and some would also go past the mountain. I must stay on the road to prevent them from crossing."

"If you stay on the road, then we also do that."

"I need you two to prevent them from jumping down from their horses and entering the forest."

"But-"

"Quick! They're coming!" Alex and Peter darted into the forest with the rifles, while James stood in the middle of the road, waiting for the demons to appear.

The demons trotted swiftly towards the mountain pass, the road getting steeper by the metre. Zetrov was in conversation with Avexor.

"Do you actually, honestly think that there will be a tra-" One bullet flew towards Avexor, but pierced Zetrov's skull instead. He fell onto the ground, dead. Avexor and Santlus both roared, seeing their dead friend.

"WHAT THE-" They both jumped down from their horses and raced forward with their automatic pistols and spears in the direction of the trees, when James suddenly swung his sword, and five soldiers crumpled in seconds. Immediately, a hail of bullets shot out of both sides of the forest, raining on top of the demons, killing around a hundred of them. However, the rest rushed into the woods and flooded onto the mountain pass. Fireballs launched into the sky and rained down onto the mountain. As James plunged sideways to avoid a flaming projectile, Alex and Peter shot randomly at the crowd of demons, trying to hold them back, but the demons kept coming, screaming, waving their weapons.

Avexor and Santlus both charged into the battle alongside theirs and Zetrov's soldiers, carrying massive, heavy battle axes made of demonic steel, which was even tougher than diorite. Five hundred demon infantry formed a Macedonian phalanx and sprinted in the direction of the mountain, and three hundred cavalry cantered behind them. James noticed the soldiers rushing past him, but he was duelling both Avexor and three of his top soldiers at once, there was no chance to stop them. But then, James had an idea. He plunged backwards and cut a tree in half with the sword. At the same time, he stabbed Avexor, and as the tree toppled down, he was forced to sidestep. Then James came at him with a roundhouse kick at Avexor's hip and then jab-punched him twice in his face as Avexor's hook punched him. But then, the soldier beside Avexor bumped into him while he was trying to avoid the falling tree, and the demon general landed beside James's feet, and he finished the demon off. After killing Avexor, James turned and sprinted in the direction of the mountains, after the eight hundred demons that had gone in that direction.

Behind James, Peter and Alex were struggling to fight the demons that had flooded into the forest. Alex had taken a spear from a demon that she'd defeated earlier and was using it as a quarterstaff, spinning it around in her hand, knocking demon soldiers off balance, but more demons took the place of their fallen comrades. Peter was shooting the enemy randomly with his rifle, meanwhile also stabbing at them with a short sword, but he had taken a few wounds on his face and legs, and the demons were rapidly overwhelming him.

Then, suddenly, Santlus realised that a part of their troops were heading over the mountain, and he screamed, "Advance! Go over the mountains! There are only three of them!" But over the din of battle, only the soldiers around him heard him, and only these two hundred or so soldiers obeyed. However, Santlus still ran with the soldiers, until he saw Avexor's body lying on the ground, with blood splattered around him.

The roar of rage that Santlus let out was deafening and echoed around the surrounding countryside. Even James turned around to see what had happened, but when he saw Santlus staring at Avexor's body, he sprinted faster in the direction of the demon soldiers, who were already on the summit of the mountain, and Santlus suddenly noticed James running towards the other side of the mountain and set out after him. Part of the demon cavalry turned around and galloped towards James instead of going over the mountain, and James suddenly had an idea: if he could jump out of the way of the charging cavalry the cavalry would crash into Santlus, but the problem was that he couldn't get out of the way in time. However, James still ran for the shelter of the forest, but when the demon cavalry was only ten metres or so away from him, he leaped upward, twisted his body in midair, grabbed one member of the cavalry, knocked him out and sat on his horse. Then, the demon cavalry smashed into Santlus, without any chance to stop.

After the cavalry slowed down, Santlus was nowhere to be seen. The soldiers looked around in confusion, searching for their leader, but when they saw James, they frowned and cantered at him. But without their generals they forgot to make a formation, not even advancing in straight lines. James saw some gaps in the charging force, and he quickly leapt into one of the gaps. As he had vanished into their midst, the demon cavalry looked around in confusion once more. Behind them, part of the infantry looked extremely confused, and began to argue with the cavalry. James took this opportunity to knock one soldier off his horse, and then he swiftly mounted it. Before anyone had realised what he had done, James had urged the horse to gallop at full speed, smashing into other horses and demons. They screamed and scattered as James finished them off from his horse; without their leader, they were foolish and stupid.

A few minutes later, James had almost killed all the cavalry and this part of the infantry, when he screamed, "Flee!" The demons in the forest also heard him and thinking that it was Santlus or Avexor that gave the order, they all ran in the direction of Gremword's palace. Suddenly, the battle was over.

After the demons had disappeared, Peter and Alex came out of the trees, holding their weapons, which were covered in blood.

"What happened? Why were they running?"

"I killed Avexor and Santlus, and then when I was battling one part of the cavalry, I had almost overcome them, which made them really panicky, and then I shouted, 'flee,' and they all ran. The demons in the forest probably also heard me shouting, and saw the running soldiers, so they joined in."

"Good thinking. So now we return to the island-base," Alex said. "It won't be easy."

"We'll manage," James said. He hoped that he spoke the truth.

The trio made camp beside a river when night fell. They refreshed themselves by drinking the freshwater and eating some fish that James caught, and they were so tired that they all instantly fell asleep. He dreamed about demons and people who were not demons but also not normal people in a battle on the beach. The people who were fighting the demons seemed to have just landed on the demons' coast, with their boats docked on the shore. However, James woke up very quickly and found that it was already morning.

Nineteen
The End (or not?)

It was strange that when they were travelling back to the shore, no demons attacked them, except for some scattered forces that were guarding their bases. In fact, the journey to the shore was quite peaceful, as they didn't have many problems except for the weather (which was sometimes bad). But when they arrived at the summit of the last small mountain that overlooked the sea, there was a huge, ferocious battle raging below, and James could clearly see that it was the battle that he had seen in the dream all those nights ago.

"How will we get past that battle? It seems to be between the demons and our base's alliance, but why are our base's soldiers here?" Alex asked.

"Before we got on the boats to come here, I asked Cordova to organise an attack force to invade the demons," James explained. "And he said yes." Alex nodded, understanding the reason why the soldiers were here. But then the battle started to turn in the demons' favour. There was a port beside the shore, and the ships docked inside it were firing cannons at the fighters! James spotted the ships and told the others, "Look! There are a few ships in a port over there! They're firing cannons at our alliance's soldiers."

"Oh no, our numbers have gotten smaller!"

James started pacing around a small area beside Peter.

"We must help them," Peter said worriedly. There might be a way to destroy the ships!"

"But how?" asked Alex. "We can't just go up there and set fire to them one by one or whatever!"

"Wait!" James suddenly said; he had just noticed something. "We don't have to set fire to them one by one; the ships are all chained together! If we set fire to one of them, then the others will burn too!"

"How will we set fire to one of them then?" Alex asked. "We can't just walk there; the demons are between us and the ships!"

"We can make a torch, and you can carry the torch to one of the ships with your wind powers, Alex," Peter suggested.

"Let's do that," James agreed.

Peter rubbed two sticks together and created a flame, while Alex swiftly used wind to carry one of the torches there. Two minutes later, one of the ships was set ablaze. Then, an army of winged people flew into the battle, shooting arrows at the demons, and they started to push them back. James didn't know who they were, but he thought that they must be the Alatueans from the Alatus base's alliance.

"That must be the Alatus base!" Alex gasped. "I've seen them before, they look like that, and they were quite friendly to us. They might have sided with our alliance in this battle!" Next, one of the soldiers from the Alatus base noticed James, and rushed toward him, calling one of his mates to come along. When they reached James, they also noticed Peter and Alex. Then one of the Alatueans spoke as he landed beside James.

"Who are you? I see that you are not a demon, but who are you?"

James stared at the Alatuean and said, "We are, um, kids from the other base's alliance, that is not the Alatus base, and my father was a Fesitte…"

"But now that I come to think of it, there is a possibility of you being an impostor, as the demons might be using you to break into one of the bases." Then, one of the demons noticed James, Peter, Alex and the Alatuean soldier, and pointed towards them, getting several other demons' attention. Twenty demons rushed towards James, Peter and Alex, but as they began to run to kill the demons, the two Alatuean soldiers picked them up and rose into the air. The demons sent a volley of arrows at the Alatueans, but they simply flew a bit higher and dodged them. None of the arrows hit the Alatueans.

Then, almost immediately, an important-looking soldier from the alliance that the Fessites were in noticed them in the air and shouted, "Hey! What do you think you're doing, Alatuean soldier, carrying three of the kids from my base in the air?"

"Oh, er…I thought that they were demon impostors or something. Sorry, sir."

"Well then, bring them down right now," he said, taking out his bow. The Alatuean soldier noticed the threat of the bow, and immediately flew behind the Alatuean lines, where an officer instantly recognised who they were.

"What are you three doing here, on the border of the Forest of Demons?"

"We just completed a quest to kill Gremword," Alex explained, "and we were successful. We also burned the ships with a torch." The officer's and the surrounding peoples' eyes all widened in surprise, and he ran off, telling everyone that they had killed Gremword.

Then, suddenly, many of the soldiers at the back of the battle ran over to congratulate them, lifting them onto their shoulders, and onto a grand ship to be taken back to their base. Even the demons hesitated for a moment to see what was happening and got stabbed the next second by the Alliances' soldiers. The news that Gremword was dead made all the people in the alliance extremely happy, and James, Peter and Alex were given the top level of hospitality on their journey back to the base. Every day on the ship there was partying, and many people wanted to hear about their adventures in the forest and the battles that they had fought.

On the day they arrived at the base, everyone lifted James, Peter and Alex onto their shoulders, everyone except for Lukas, Ryan and some of their friends. After being carried into the base, they had an enormous, grand feast even though it was not lunchtime yet and had a party for the rest of the day. James told several people about his adventures in the forest, and he lounged in his room, thinking about all the events that happened in the last few weeks. In the afternoon, he went out of his room again and played with his friends for the rest of the day, until sunset, when they had a campfire right outside the dining pergola. They sang songs merrily and chatted, until many kids were yawning and tired, so they went to bed. James and Peter stayed up until it was very late but finally went to bed around eleven. For James, that single

185

day went extremely quickly, but he was very tired. He fell asleep just as his head touched his sleeping bag.

However, all around the base, the massive Iceshield ocean was quiet; the base's campfire and the rising moon were the only lights that were to be seen for over a hundred kilometres. The moonlight shone onto the peaceful ocean, dimly lighting the waves, above the Iceshield ocean were several seagulls, calmly flying around. But then, on the dark stretch of water that was right above the teleporter connecting the past and the future, the Iceshield ocean began to shake, as if an earthquake was starting.

Then, suddenly, the teleporter on the ocean bed exploded, causing enormous tidal waves to flow in all directions. The faint form of an enormous snake became visible right beneath the water, and suddenly, the unmistakable figure of Gremword erupted out of the water. In his right hand he held a mighty, golden sword, and in his left hand there was James's father, the Fesittes' commander. He was unconscious and his breathing was faint; he was almost dead. Gremword's eyes were bulging, his nostrils were flaring, and his fangs showed. He let out a deafening roar that rattled the air around him and made the ocean tremble in fright.

"So, this is the future! James must be here! Wherever you are, James, I will get you and destroy your entire base! Then the demons will rule, and you will **NEVER BE HEARD OF AGAIN!**"

To be continued...